THE PAINTED LADY

A LT. KATE GAZZARA STORY

BLAIR HOWARD

For Frances, my beautiful granddaughter.

1

GALLERY OF DEATH

THE CALL CAME IN AT 7:23 AM ON A CRISP APRIL MORNING, just as I was finishing my second cup of coffee and watching Samson demolish his breakfast with his characteristic enthusiasm. You know how some dogs pick at their food? Not Samson. When that bowl hits the floor, it's like watching a furry tornado in action. All one hundred and fifteen pounds of German Shepherd focused on one simple task: making that kibble disappear.

I was still in my robe, hair pulled back in a messy ponytail, enjoying the rare luxury of a slow morning. Tuesday was supposed to be my late day, one of the few perks of being a homicide captain. But as anyone who's spent time in law enforcement knows, dead bodies don't follow your schedule.

"Good morning, Captain," Tracy Ramirez's voice crackled through my radio, cutting through the peaceful morning like a knife. "We have a body at Reynolds Gallery, Southside. I'm there now. It looks like suicide, but something about it feels off to me."

Something feels off. Tracy had been working homicide

long enough to trust her instincts, and when she said something felt off, it usually meant we were dealing with more than met the eye.

"I'll be there as quickly as I can," I replied. "In the meantime, make sure the scene is secured."

I showered, dressed quickly in jeans, a white top and tan leather jacket, grabbed my badge and gun from the kitchen counter, where I'd left them the night before, a habit that would probably horrify the department's safety instructors.

"Sorry, boy," I said to Samson as I clipped his leash. "Looks like our quiet morning just ended."

Samson's ears perked up immediately. He knows the difference between a grocery store run and a crime scene call, and his whole demeanor shifted from lazy slob to alert K-9. The dog had been my partner for a little over three years now, and he'd become as essential to my work as my badge or weapon.

As we headed for my unmarked SUV, I tried to remember what I knew about the Reynolds Gallery. It wasn't much. I'd driven past it dozens of times during my regular patrols through the Southside arts district, but it wasn't the kind of place that usually generated police calls. The Southside had transformed dramatically over the past decade, evolving from a collection of abandoned warehouses and industrial buildings into Chattanooga's premier arts destination.

The transformation hadn't been without controversy, though. Longtime residents complained about rising rents and the loss of affordable housing, while city planners praised the economic development and cultural revitalization. Both sides had valid points, but my job wasn't urban planning; it was dealing with the consequences when people's lives intersected with homicidal violence.

The Reynolds Gallery was at the heart of the arts district, occupying what had once been a textile warehouse. The building's industrial bones remained visible—exposed brick walls, high ceilings with steel beams, polished concrete floors —but everything else screamed upscale gallery. Large windows displayed carefully curated local and regional artwork, and even from the street, you could tell this wasn't a place where you'd find velvet Elvis paintings or dogs playing poker.

The scene outside buzzed with controlled chaos. Patrol officers had cordoned off the area with yellow tape, creating a perimeter that kept the growing crowd of curious onlookers at a safe distance. Paramedics stood by their ambulance, officially present in case someone needed medical attention, but more likely because protocol required their presence at any scene involving a dead body.

I noticed Samson's immediate reaction as we approached the gallery entrance. The dog's hackles rose along his spine, and a low growl rumbled deep in his chest—not the playful growl he used when we wrestled at home, but the serious, warning growl that meant danger.

In my three years of working with Samson, I'd learned to trust his instincts completely. Dogs perceive things we miss: scents we can't detect, sounds we can't hear, subtle changes in human behavior that escape our notice. When Samson reacted like that, something was definitely not right.

"What do we have?" I asked Officer Martinez who had been first on scene. Martinez was a solid cop, nine years on the force, the kind of officer who paid attention to details and followed procedures without getting bogged down in bureaucracy.

"Lisa Reynolds, thirty-four, gallery owner," Martinez replied, consulting his notebook. "Found dead at her desk by her assistant, who came in early to prep for an exhibition opening. Single gunshot wound to the right temple. Small caliber pistol on the floor next to her chair. No signs of forced entry, doors were locked from the inside when the assistant arrived."

Sergeant Tracy Ramirez, a divorced mother of two teenage girls, was in her late forties. She was tall; not as tall as me, but enough to cut an imposing figure. Her jet-black hair had not a streak of gray, and although she carried a few extra pounds, they didn't detract from her overall good looks. She'd been a cop almost as long as I had. She was tough, thorough, and reliable, which is why she was on my team.

She joined me a moment later, and together we studied the scene through the gallery's front window before entering. "It looks… staged to me," she muttered.

The mortal remains of Lisa Reynolds were in her office, slumped in her chair at an antique wooden desk positioned in front of the window, and surrounded by carefully lit paintings and sculptures. Her long auburn hair partially obscured the wound, and a small, nickel-plated pistol lay on the polished concrete floor beside her chair.

"You're right, Tracy," I said. "It looks too neat, too arranged. Real life is messier than this. When people decide to end their lives, especially with a firearm, there's usually more evidence of the internal struggle that led to the decision. This scene looks like something staged for a photograph. Come on, let's go take a look." And together, we went inside, and into Lisa's office.

Two minutes later we were joined by Mike Willis, our CSI supervisor. Willis was a short, overweight man with enormous hands that looked like they should belong to someone who worked construction or hauled freight. He'd been at his job longer than I'd been a cop.

"I've only been here about twenty minutes, Kate," he said. "Single gunshot wound to the right temple. Small caliber, probably a .22 or .25. But there's something…" He paused, studying Samson's continued agitation. "Your partner there seems to think we're missing something."

I nodded. "You'll check for GSR, right?" I asked, watching as Samson refused to approach the desk where Lisa's body sat. Instead, he circled the perimeter of the gallery, his nose working overtime, occasionally stopping to sniff specific spots on the floor or walls. *Someone's been here, and recently*, I thought.

Mike gave me one of those 'what d'you think' looks.

I grinned at him and said, "Has anyone checked that back room yet?" I asked, pointing toward a door at the rear of the gallery to which Samson kept returning.

"Not yet. I've been waiting for you to clear the main scene first."

Smart man. Willis had been doing this longer than most of us had been breathing, and he knew better than to rush things. Crime scenes told stories, but only if you took the time to read them carefully.

Corbin Russell, my official partner, arrived just as I was snapping on a pair of latex gloves and, after a perfunctory, "Good morning, Cap," he immediately set about documenting the scene with photographs and detailed notes. I smiled and shook my head.

Corbin was in his late thirties, with the kind of steady demeanor that came from deep religious faith and a genuine belief in justice. He didn't drink much, rarely cursed, and approached every investigation with the same "just the facts" mentality that made him both reliable and often irritating. But he was thorough in ways that often saved cases.

"No suicide note," he observed, photographing the desk area from multiple angles. "The victim's positioned naturally in her chair, gun on the floor consistent with having dropped from her right hand. But..." He paused, studying the scene more carefully. "The blood spatter pattern seems inconsistent with the contact wound."

That was Corbin, always catching details that others missed. But as I watched Samson's continued agitated wanderings, I wasn't convinced about the natural positioning. It told me there were layers to this scene that we hadn't uncovered yet.

"What is it, Sammy?" I whispered as he looked plaintively up at me. And he turned, took a few steps, stopped, and looked back at me.

"Okay," I said. "Show me."

Samson led me toward the storage room behind the main gallery space, his nose practically glued to the floor. Inside the small room, I could see dust patterns that suggested some of the contents had recently been disturbed. I furrowed my brow as I stared at the polished concrete floor. There were two scuff marks. *Someone's been in here*, I thought. Samson was all over the room. Could it be that someone had been hiding in here, waiting and watching?

"Hey, Corbin, get Willis back here," I called. "Samson's found something."

While Willis processed the storage room, Tony Cooper arrived and began his quiet canvassing of the neighboring galleries and studios. Tony was our newest detective, promoted from patrol just three years earlier, but he had a natural gift for making people comfortable. At six feet three and built like a linebacker, you'd expect him to intimidate witnesses. Instead, they seemed to trust him instinctively.

Maybe it was because Tony never pushed, never pressured. He asked questions as if he was genuinely curious about the answers, not as if he was trying to catch someone in a lie. In a community like the arts district, where people tended to be suspicious of authority, Tony's approach was invaluable.

"What ya got, Tony?" I asked when he entered the room a little less than an hour later.

"Several people mentioned tension between her and her artists over pricing," he reported, his notebook filled with careful cursive handwriting. "I get the impression she was a tough negotiator, maybe tougher than some people expected, or liked. And there's something else; a missing person case. An art student named Sophia Blake disappeared three weeks ago. Apparently, Blake had been asking questions about Lisa's authentication practices."

Missing persons and mysterious deaths have a way of connecting in my experience. When someone disappears and then people start dying, it's usually not a coincidence.

"Did anyone hear the gunshot?" I asked.

"Nah," Tony replied. "This old place..." He looked up at the high ceiling. "Thick walls and the building next door has a loading dock where they start deliveries around 6 AM. Hydraulic lifts, metal on concrete, small caliber gunshot. Nobody heard it."

I nodded and said, "Stick with it, Tony. You never know."

By then, Tracy had taken charge of interviewing the gallery staff and early witnesses. She, too, had a gift for getting people to open up, probably developed during years of being a divorced mother of two teenage girls. If you could handle all that teenage drama, you sure as hell could handle a bunch of snooty gallery employees.

"Lisa was demanding but fair," I heard Jenny Walsh, the assistant who'd found the body, say. Jenny was maybe twenty-five, with nervous hands and the kind of pale complexion that suggested she spent most of her time indoors. "She expected a lot from everyone," she continued, "including herself. But lately she'd been stressed about something. Kept checking her phone during meetings, seemed nervous about appointments. And she was really upset about that student who'd been asking questions, Sophia Blake."

There was that name again, Sophia Blake.

"What questions?" Tracy asked.

"You know, authentication stuff. Provenance documentation. Where some of the pieces in the gallery had come from, how we verified their age and authenticity. Lisa said the girl was naïve, didn't understand how the art business really worked." She paused, wrapped her arms around herself, and then continued. "But she seemed worried, not just annoyed. Like maybe the questions were bothering her somehow."

"D'you know if Lisa owned a gun?" I asked.

Jenny shook her head. "Not that I know of. She could have, I suppose."

It meant nothing. It wasn't something a woman would do, flash a gun around, not in my opinion. And if Lisa didn't own a gun, where had the pistol come from?

At around ten o'clock, a representative from the Hunter Museum of American Art arrived. She'd been sent to assess any potential damage to the museum's artwork on loan to the gallery. *Geez*, I thought. *Word does quickly get around.*

The conservator was probably in her late fifties, tall, with a round face, gray eyes, carefully coifed hair and an air of both authority and genuine concern.

She introduced herself. "I'm Dr. Patricia Whitman," she said, holding out her hand. "Are you in charge here?"

I nodded. "Captain Gazzara," I said, shaking her hand. "How can I help you, Dr. Whitman?"

"I need to take a look around at our artwork to make sure there's no damage, if that's all right with you."

"I'm sorry, Doctor," I said. "This is an active investigation. And—"

"I won't get in the way, I promise," she said, cutting me off.

Again, I shook my head. "I'm sorry, Doctor. How about I have Officer Martinez call you when we're clear? In the meantime, I'd like a few words, if I may."

We talked for several minutes about her job and her concerns about the exhibits. She was also quite taken with Samson.

"What a beautiful dog," she said. "Is it all right if I pet him? He won't bite me, will he?"

I smiled and nodded. Samson, usually wary of strangers, seemed happy to have her scratch him behind his ears, something he rarely did with people he didn't know.

"Such a tragedy," Dr. Whitman said softly, eyeing the gallery's collection. "Lisa dealt in some significant pieces. She had an eye for quality, even if her business practices were sometimes... well, a little aggressive. I hope this doesn't affect the integrity of the works."

"So you knew her well, then?" I asked.

She shrugged. "As well as you can know anybody, I suppose," she replied thoughtfully. "It was more of a business thing rather than a friendship. It's so sad. I just can't understand why she would shoot herself. I mean, she seemed to have everything going for her, and..." she trailed off and shook her head, seemingly lost in thought.

"Hey, Captain," Tony said, interrupting my own thoughts. "Mike needs you when you have a minute."

"Tell him I'll be with him as soon as I can," I said, then turned again to Whitman. "Dr...." I began and, over the next twenty minutes, I continued to question her at some length, trying to get a feel for the world she and Lisa lived and worked in. Her knowledge of art authentication and the local art scene proved invaluable as I tried to understand Lisa's business relationships. She explained the complex world of art provenance, authentication certificates, and the sometimes murky process of determining whether a piece was genuine or fake.

"How do you tell if a piece is authentic, Dr. Whitman?"

"That's a question to which there are many answers, Captain," she replied. "Authentication is both art and science," she explained. "You need to understand historical techniques, paint chemistry, canvas aging, even the kinds of nails and fasteners used in different time periods. It's a specialized field, and there aren't many people qualified to do it properly."

Geez, I thought.

"Well, that's all for now, Dr. Whitman," I said finally, offering her my hand. "Thank you for your help. I'm sure we'll want to tap your expertise again, so if you'll give your number to my partner, Sergeant Russell over there, I'd appreciate it." I turned away and motioned for Corbin.

It was then, as I was about to go see what Mike Willis wanted, that the morning's calm was shattered.

Marcus Webb, a wealthy and well-respected collector, had somehow managed to slip past the police perimeter and burst into the gallery, demanding to speak with Lisa about some 'fraudulent pieces' she'd sold him.

Webb was a hefty man in his early forties, impeccably dressed despite the early hour, but his composure was cracking around the edges.

Samson immediately positioned himself between me and Webb, as if sensing the man's agitation and potential for violence. The dog's protective instincts had saved my life more than once, and I'd learned to pay attention when he went into protective mode.

Well, now, I thought. *What have we here?* Webb's aggressive behavior and obvious financial motive made him an immediate person of interest. He was red-faced, sweating despite the cool morning air, and his hands were clenched into fists.

Chapter 1

"Who are you?" he yelled. "Are you the police? Are you here to arrest Lisa? If not, you should. Look, I need to speak to her. She sold me three pieces last month. I paid her over $300,000 only to discover the paintings are sophisticated forgeries. I've been demanding a refund, threatening legal action. She keeps putting me off, claiming they were authentic, saying I didn't understand the authentication process. But NO MORE!" he shouted. And every head in the gallery turned to look at him.

Three hundred thousand dollars. Now that was serious money, the kind that made people do serious things. Webb went on to describe his attempts to get his money back, his increasingly frustrated encounters with Lisa, and veiled threats about "making her pay" for what he saw as deliberate fraud.

"When did you last speak with Ms. Reynolds?" I asked.

"Yesterday afternoon. I called her around four, told her I was done playing games. I told her if she didn't make this right, I'd find another way to get satisfaction."

I didn't have a time of death yet, but as soon as I did, Webb's alibi would need checking. His motive was clear, and his opportunity? Who knew? Plus his obvious anger; that he might be capable of violence wouldn't surprise me.

"Do you own any firearms, Mr. Webb?" I asked.

"Of course I do. Several. I'm a collector..." He paused, realizing the implications. "What? She's dead, isn't she? Are you out of your mind? I didn't... I would never..."

"I'm sure you wouldn't, Mr. Webb," I said, but we'll need to check to see if the weapon was registered to him and if it was, well, he would have some explaining to do.

Doc Sheddon, the Hamilton County Medical Examiner, arrived about fifteen minutes after Webb left at a little after ten-thirty. He waddled through the gallery entrance with his characteristic unhurried gait, his large black medical bag hanging heavily in his right hand. The small man was puffing slightly from the exertion, his round face already sporting that inappropriately jovial expression that always reminded me of Bilbo Baggins.

"Kate Gazzara," he said, adjusting his half-glasses as he surveyed the scene. "You brought coffee, I hope. No? Oh dear. Oh well. So, what do we have here?"

"Apparent suicide by gunshot, Doc," I said. "Single wound to the right temple. Small caliber pistol on the floor beside the chair."

"Doctor Gazzara, is it now?" he asked sarcastically. "Well, we'll see, won't we," he said as he walked over to the body with surprising grace for someone of his build. Despite being in his late fifties, overweight, and almost completely bald, he was surprisingly fit, and also my friend.

"Single gunshot wound to the right temple," he observed, pulling on latex gloves. "The entry wound is consistent with a small-caliber firearm. But let me take a closer look at the trajectory and powder burns."

Doc bent over Lisa's body, examining the wound with a magnifying glass. He studied the angle, the surrounding tissue, and the absence, or presence, of gunshot residue.

"This is interesting," he said after several minutes. "The wound angle suggests the shot came from slightly above and in front of the victim, not the typical angle for self-inflicted wounds."

"Suicide?" I asked, though I already suspected the answer.

"Unlikely," Doc said as he moved around the body, examining it from different angles. "Looking at the trajectory. Most people who shoot themselves in the temple press the gun directly against the skin. The stippling around the wound indicates the shot was fired from eighteen to twenty-four inches away."

He opened his medical bag, rummaged around inside,

then, unable to find what he was looking for, turned to me and said, "No contact burns, minimal gunshot residue on the palms of her hands. Which would indicate she was in a defensive posture."

"How minimal?" Corbin asked, joining our conversation.

"Not enough for someone who fired the weapon," Doc replied without hesitation. "The pattern suggests she may have tried to deflect the gun, but she didn't fire it herself."

Doc Sheddon continued his preliminary examination, checking for other signs of trauma or evidence of restraint. "No obvious defensive wounds. Hmm, interesting." He lowered his chin and stared at the body over his glasses. "Death would have been instantaneous. Single shot to the brain. She wouldn't have suffered."

He stood back, removing his gloves with practiced efficiency. "I'll know more after the autopsy, but this has all the characteristics of a staged suicide. Someone wanted Lisa Reynolds dead, and they tried to make it look like she did it herself."

"Time of death?" I asked.

"Give me a minute," he said, then took a meat thermometer from his bag, and said, "Help me lift her into a sitting position, would you, please?"

I did as he asked and watched as he lifted her blouse and inserted the thermometer under her ribcage and into the liver. He waited for a few seconds, then said, "Based on the liver temperature and rigor, sometime between six and seven this morning."

"That's consistent with her assistant finding her around seven-fifteen," I muttered.

"Hey, y'all. Okay if I come in?"

I turned to see Jack North standing in the doorway. I looked at Doc. He nodded.

"Come on in, Jack," I said, without turning round.

Jack was my computer forensics specialist, a somewhat reformed problem child who'd found his calling in digital investigation. He had the kind of technical skills that made up for his occasionally difficult personality.

He walked across to the desk, grabbed Lisa's laptop, and I followed him as he walked back out into the gallery, sat down at the receptionist's desk, and tapped the spacebar. And, much to Jack's relief, the screen lit up to show a desktop filled with folders.

"No lock screen," he muttered as he accessed the gallery's security system.

The security footage showed Lisa arriving alone that morning around six-twenty-two and no one entering or leaving through the front entrance after that. But digital evidence could be manipulated, and the footage didn't cover the entire gallery, only the main gallery and the front door. If someone had been hiding in the storage room overnight, they certainly didn't appear on camera.

"The system's pretty basic," Jack reported. "Motion-activated cameras cover the main entrance and gallery floor, but nothing in the back rooms or storage areas. Whoever planned this knew the limitations of the security setup."

Willis' ballistics analysis of the gun and wound would take time, but his preliminary findings were already raising questions. "Weapon's a .25 caliber automatic. And the gun's been wiped clean. No fingerprints."

Hah! People who commit suicide don't typically wipe their fingerprints off the weapon afterward.

As the morning progressed, additional people from the arts community stopped by, most significant of whom were Carmen Rodriguez, Lisa's business insurance agent, and a young woman by the name of Grace Parker wanting to ask questions for her art.

Grace was young, maybe twenty-eight, with the kind of

earnest intensity that journalism schools breed into their students. She'd been tracking what she called "suspicious patterns" in local art sales.

"Too many high-value pieces appearing with convenient gaps in their provenance... you know? The ownership history," Grace explained. "I'm sure you know, paintings that disappeared during World War II and suddenly reappear with authentication certificates but no clear chain of custody. Or pieces that were supposedly damaged in house fires but show up perfectly preserved a few years later."

Carmen Rodriguez had noticed similar patterns. "We've had an unusual number of claims related to art authentication disputes," she told me. "People buying expensive pieces, then discovering they're not what they thought they were. It usually takes months or even years for buyers to figure out they've been defrauded, usually when they try to get the piece insured. We always carry out an extensive examination before we issue a policy," she explained.

I found both Carmen and Grace interesting, and talked to both of them for a few minutes, but with a crime scene to deal with, I got rid of them both as quickly as I could without being rude, I hoped, promising to talk to them in-depth when I had more time.

I spent most of the rest of the morning working the crime scene, for crime scene it was now that Doc had handed down his verdict. And then, at almost noon, I received a call from the chief demanding my presence in his office ASAP.

⸻

CHRISTY, Chief Johnston's PA, was nowhere to be seen when I arrived in his outer office, so I knocked on the door and walked in.

"Kate," he said, looking up from his computer screen.

"Take a seat. Tell me about Lisa Reynolds. And before you begin, you should understand that she was well-connected in the art community," he said, his white mustache bristling with each word. "The district represents millions of dollars in city investment and tourism revenue. If this becomes a scandal about art fraud, it could embarrass the city and do irreparable damage to our cultural reputation."

Translation: Don't screw this up, Kate, and try to keep the media focused on the murder rather than any underlying business irregularities. It wasn't the first time I'd been warned about such things, and it wouldn't be the last.

"Understood, Chief. We're treating it as a homicide and following the leads."

He stared at me for a long moment, then nodded and turned back to his computer, and so ended possibly the shortest interview I'd had with him in my twenty-five years on the force.

"Good," he said without looking up. "Keep me informed of any developments, especially if this expands beyond a single death."

And I got out of there wondering why the hell he'd seen the need to waste my time like that. I stood for a moment in the hall outside his outer office, trying to figure out what to do next. I was still only hours into the investigation, so I decided to grab a sandwich and go back to the scene.

"Come on, Sammy," I muttered. "I think the old goat is losing it."

By mid-afternoon, I had more questions than answers, but the shape of something larger was beginning to emerge. Willis's preliminary analysis confirmed the gunshot was not self-inflicted, and the weapon had been wiped clean.

"I'm almost certain someone was waiting for her in that storage room," Willis explained, showing me photographs of microscopic evidence. "Though how they got in, I can't say.

There's no sign of forced entry at the rear entrance, so I'd say whoever it was must have had a key. It looks amateurish to me. Maybe a heat of the moment thing, and they decided to make it look like suicide, but they made so many mistakes it's easy to prove otherwise."

By four o'clock, I was liking Marcus Webb for it. The financial motive was obvious. The man had lost hundreds of thousands of dollars to what he believed were forgeries sold to him through Lisa's gallery. And as a gun collector, he'd have both access to weapons and knowledge of how to use them.

"Run the gun's registration for me, will you, Mike?" I asked.

He nodded, told me he'd let me know, then went back about his business.

But the staging bothered me. Webb was angry and desperate, but I couldn't see a man like him hiding out in a storage room but, as they say, 'There's nothing as strange as folks.' *So who knows?* I thought.

By then, Jack was back at the office, so I called him and asked him to research Sophia Blake's background—the missing graduate student—and then I asked Tracy to investigate Lisa's business dealings. I couldn't shake the feeling that Samson had been trying to tell me something important about the crime scene. The big dog's instincts had never been wrong before. *If only he could talk*, I thought wistfully.

The afternoon brought additional complications when Vincent Harper, a freelance art authenticator who'd worked with Lisa's gallery, was also reported missing by his office manager. Harper had been scheduled for appointments that morning but never showed up, and no one could reach him by phone.

"Geez, two missing persons connected to the same

gallery, and a homicide," Tracy observed. "That can't be a coincidence."

Ryan Mitchell, a former gallery employee, arrived voluntarily to provide information about Lisa's business practices. Mitchell had been fired three months earlier after discovering what he called "irregularities" in inventory records.

"Lisa was running some kind of side business," Mitchell explained. "Pieces would appear in the gallery overnight, get photographed and documented, then disappear again without any sales records. When I started asking questions, she fired me and threatened legal action if I discussed her business practices with anyone."

Father Michael Blake arrived in the late afternoon, concerned about several young artists from his youth program who worked part-time at local galleries. The priest's genuine worry for his students provided another perspective on the arts community.

"These kids are vulnerable," Father Blake explained. "They're passionate about art but naïve about business. If someone's exploiting that passion for illegal purposes, it could destroy their futures."

By late afternoon, the pieces of a complex puzzle were scattered across Chattanooga's art community. Samson, whenever he was in the gallery, still seemed agitated. The apparent murder, the missing persons cases suggested a pattern of violence, and the art fraud angle opened up motives involving hundreds of thousands of dollars.

Standing in the gallery as the late afternoon light filtered through the large windows, casting long shadows across the carefully arranged artwork, I made a mental note to look deeper into Sophia Blake's disappearance and its connection to authentication fraud. Missing art students, missing art authenticators, and dead gallery owners didn't happen in the same small community by coincidence.

The chief was right; the financial stakes for the city were enormous. But more importantly, someone had committed murder and tried to make it look like suicide. In my book, that made them both a killer and a coward.

The question was whether our killer was a professional or just someone with a grudge.

Either way, they'd made mistakes. And in my experience, people who make mistakes usually make more of them.

The hunt was on.

2

THE SCULPTOR'S END

It was two days after Lisa Reynolds' death, at six-forty-seven in the morning, and I was at home reviewing case files over my morning coffee when my phone rang. I checked the screen. It was Tracy. *Damn it!* I thought. At that hour in the morning, it could only be bad news, and it was.

I flipped the screen and took the call.

"We've got another body," she said, almost matter-of-factly. "Jake Williams, sculptor. Found dead in his loft studio on Broad Street. This one's definitely not suicide."

I sighed and shook my head. "Any connection to Lisa Reynolds?" I asked.

"Don't know yet. I just got here. I've notified the others, including Mike and Doc Sheddon. You coming?"

"Y...ep!" I drew it out and popped the P. "Text me the address, then make sure the scene is locked down. I'll be there as soon as I can."

I hung up, swallowed the dregs of my coffee, grabbed my badge, Glock and jacket and headed for the door. Samson beat me to it, as he always does. He was already at the door by the time I grabbed my keys.

Chapter 2

The drive to Jake Williams' converted warehouse loft took me through the heart of Chattanooga's revitalized downtown. The sculptor had chosen a building that perfectly embodied the city's transformation from industrial past to artistic future. Large windows flooded the space with natural light, ideal for someone working with clay and stone.

I'd heard Jake's name mentioned during the Reynolds investigation. Apparently, he'd done some restoration work for Lisa's gallery. Now he was dead, and my gut was telling me the two cases were connected. Coincidences in a homicide investigation are about as rare as unicorns.

The building was one of those converted warehouses that developers love—high ceilings, exposed brick, plenty of character. Most of the structure was commercial space, but a handful of people lived in converted space on the lower floors. Jake's studio occupied the entire third floor, accessible by an industrial elevator or a narrow staircase that climbed along the building's exterior wall.

Outside the building, Mike Willis was already unloading his equipment, his shiny bald head gleaming in the early morning sun. "Morning, Kate. This one's messier than your gallery scene. The victim's on the third floor. No signs of forced entry on the main entrance, but somebody got in somehow, that's for sure."

For some reason I can't remember, I decided to take the stairs, and so did Mike, hefting a large black case. Samson paused on the second-floor landing, sniffing intently around the elevator gate. His nose worked overtime, cataloging scents that told a story that meant something to him, but one I couldn't read.

"What is it, boy?" I asked, following his lead to a section of the concrete landing where a small patch of dried blood was barely visible against the gray surface.

"It's fresh," Willis said. "Could be the killer's or the vic's. A preliminary blood match will give us the answer. It will take me a day or two."

"Why would he take the stairs?" I asked. "The elevator would have been easier, surely."

Willis shrugged. "The killer?" he asked. "Who knows?"

Officer Martinez met us at the third-floor entrance to Jake's studio. "The building's secure now, Captain. We've had uniforms checking every floor and interviewing the few residents who are home."

Jake Williams lay among his sculptures, sculpting tools scattered around his body as if he'd been working when attacked. But Willis's trained eye immediately identified the problems with that scenario.

"The tools were placed post-mortem," he explained, kneeling beside the body. "Look at the blood patterns. The victim was killed over here, near the door, then moved to this position among his work. The killer wanted this to look like a robbery gone wrong; they must have known about Williams' work habits and studio layout."

Jake Williams had been twenty-nine years old, according to his driver's license. He was tall, maybe six-two, with the kind of build that came from physical work—broad shoulders, powerful hands, the muscle definition of someone who lifted heavy materials regularly. His hands were stained with clay and chemical residues. He was clearly someone who worked with his materials every day.

Corbin was already there documenting the scene when we arrived. "There are defensive wounds on the victim's hands," he observed, photographing the injuries.

But there was something else about Jake's hands that caught my attention. The chemical stains weren't just from clay and typical sculpting materials. There were darker discolorations that suggested exposure to acids and other compounds not normally used in contemporary sculpture.

"Corbin, what do you make of the weapon of choice?" I asked, studying the sculpting tool that had been used to kill Jake.

"A riffler," he replied, eyeing the bloody, slim, double-ended tool lying on the floor a few feet from the victim. "Kind of intimate, using the guy's own tools, don't you think?"

"Yeah," Mike said. "Whoever it was knew their way around."

"What's that over there?" I asked, staring at a large, free-standing cupboard.

"The artist's toolshed," Mike said with a grin. "It's quite something."

I stepped over to it, pulled open the doors and looked inside. Mike was right. It was full of sculptor's tools and a lot of other equipment that seemed unusual for a contemporary sculptor: chemicals, canvas preparation materials, paint solvents, even paints and pigments.

"This isn't the workspace of a sculptor," I muttered, examining the materials more closely.

"You're right about that," Willis said as he joined me at the cupboard. "Many of these chemicals are restricted. You need special licenses to purchase some of these compounds. They're used in professional art conservation and restoration."

"Restoration!" I muttered, more to myself than to Willis. "Mike, this guy's public persona was that of a contemporary sculptor, but this... This tells a different story. It suggests he was also into art restoration."

"That, or something else," Mike replied.

"Like what?" I asked.

"I wouldn't even like to speculate," he replied.

"You're not being helpful, Mike," I replied, slightly frustrated. I heaved a sigh and turned away from the cupboard to see Tony standing in the doorway.

"Hey, Coop, I want you to canvas the building," I called out. "Find out what Jake's neighbors heard and when. And get the contact information of anyone who visited regularly."

"On it," he said, and turned away and left, only to return a few moments later.

"Captain," he called from the door. "You got a minute?"

I stepped out into the small hallway that led to the service elevator and the stairs to find Cooper with a classy-looking woman I figured to be in her mid-thirties.

"This is Sarah Marshall," Cooper said. "She lives in the apartment directly below this one. I thought you should hear what she has to say for yourself. Ms. Marshall, this is Captain Gazzara. She's in charge of the..." he trailed off, obviously not knowing how much more to reveal.

"Ms. Marshall," I said, offering her my hand. "What can you tell me about Jake Williams and what happened last night?"

She bit her lip, thought for a moment, then said, "Well, as... he said." She glanced at Cooper. "Sorry, I forgot your name. I live in the unit below Jake's. I'm a graphic designer, you see, so I work from home. He works late most nights. Lots of noise, you know, from power tools and such. But he was considerate, usually stopped by ten PM. Last night was different, though. These old places; they're not very sound-proof. Anyway, I heard voices. It was a little after ten, not that late, really."

"Is that unusual?" I asked.

She shrugged. "It's happened before."

"You said voices," I said.

"It was muffled. I couldn't hear what they were saying, but I could hear Jake's voice, and someone else. I couldn't tell if it was a man or woman from down there, but they seemed to be arguing about something. Anyway, they stopped yelling at each other at about eleven. After that, it was quiet."

That suggested Jake had known his killer—if killer it was —and had probably let the person in willingly. The lack of forced entry tended to support that theory.

She had little more of interest to say, so I let her go, then turned to Cooper and said, "Anything else?"

"Nah, there are only three other residents. One's an elderly man named Robert Sherman. He also lives on the second floor, but he heard nothing. The other two were out."

So, someone had arrived at or about ten o'clock, spent about an hour in Jake's studio, then left. Whether Jake was dead when they left remained to be determined. With that in mind, I went to find Tracy. I found her at the bottom of the stairs seated on a bench, her laptop open on her knee, connected to the internet via her personal hotspot. She was doing a deep dive into the connection between Jake Williams and Lisa Reynolds.

"So there was one," I said.

"Boy howdy," she replied. "They were in a romantic relationship. Look at this." She turned the computer so I could see it. The two had a joint social media account going back over two years.

"And get this," Tracy said, looking up at me. "It was more than just romance. They were in business together. Jake was doing specialized work for Lisa's gallery, restoration. That's kind of odd for someone who's primarily a sculptor, don't you think?"

I thought the social media evidence painted quite a picture. The couple appeared at gallery openings together, took vacations to art museums in other cities, and Jake frequently posted photos of the restoration projects he was working on.

But Tracy's financial analysis revealed something more

interesting. "Jake's been receiving large payments from Lisa's gallery," she continued. "Ten to fifteen thousand dollars monthly, which is way above the market rate for restoration work."

That kind of money suggested Jake's services were more valuable than simple restoration. Either Lisa was overpaying him because of their romantic relationship, or Jake was providing something worth more than his public work suggested.

And the relationship angle opened up several interesting new possibilities. Love triangles, business partnerships gone wrong, shared secrets that someone wanted buried. In my experience, when romantic partners died within days of each other, something was rotten in the state of Denmark.

I was still downstairs with Tracy when the investigation took a dramatic turn; Sophia Blake's thesis advisor, Professor David Patterson, arrived at the scene at around ten-thirty. Patterson was in his mid-forties, with the slightly rumpled appearance of someone who spent more time thinking than grooming. His brown hair was unkempt, his clothes looked like they'd been slept in, and his hands shook as he spoke.

"I heard about Jake on Channel 7," he explained. "You're obviously in charge here. This can't be a coincidence, can it? First Lisa, now Jake, and Sophia still missing. What's going on?"

Samson's reaction to Patterson wasn't exactly encouraging. On Patterson's arrival, he positioned himself protectively between me and the professor, his hackles slightly raised. That level of wariness from Samson usually meant something wasn't quite right about the person.

"I'm Captain Gazzara," I said. "This is Sergeant Tracy Ramirez, and you are...?"

"Oh... Yes, of course. I'm so sorry. I'm Professor Patterson, Sophia's counselor and—"

"And your relationship to Jake Williams?" I asked as Corbin joined us.

"Good friends," he replied quickly. "We were good friends," he repeated. "I've known him for years. Wonderful artist. Wonderful. His work; quite exquisite."

"Artist?" I asked. "Sculptor or painter?"

"Both, actually," he replied. "Wonderful sculptor. More restorer than painter, though. Beautiful work. Beautiful."

"And what d'you know about his relationship with Lisa Reynolds?" I asked.

"Well," he said, tilting his head first to one side then the other. "They were lovers, weren't they? Didn't make any bones about it. Could be embarrassing at times, but there you are. Which is why I ask, the two deaths can't be a coincidence, can they?"

I ignored the question. Instead, I asked him, "What exactly was Sophia researching?"

"She was very interested in authentication; paintings, you know?" he replied. "She was researching authentication practices." Patterson was becoming more agitated. Samson backed up, closer to me, so his backside was touching my thigh. "She'd identified several suspicious pieces and was documenting inconsistencies in their provenance. She was particularly concerned about work coming through Lisa Reynolds' gallery."

"Dr. Patterson, where were you last night between ten and eleven?" I asked.

"At the university. Working late in my lab. I often stay until midnight or later when I'm analyzing samples." He paused, wiping sweat from his forehead despite the cool morning air. Then, he seemed to realize my intent. "You..." he lowered his chin and narrowed his eyes. "You don't... Surely you don't think I had anything to do with... this? You can check the keycard records."

We would of course. But keycard records could be manipulated, and Patterson clearly had the skills to do it.

"Other than your being friends, what kind of relationship did you have with Jake Williams?" Corbin asked.

"I'm sorry," he said. "Who are you?"

"He's Sergeant Russell," I said. "Please answer the question."

"Outside of our friendship, professional consultation. Jake sometimes brought me samples for analysis when he was trying to determine the age or authenticity of materials. He was one of the few local artists who understood the science behind authentication."

The more we learned about Jake's expertise, the clearer it became that he'd been involved in something far more complex than simple sculpture.

"Well, Professor," I said. "If there's anything you can think of that might be helpful, please call me." And I handed him my card and, followed by Corbin and Samson, I walked back up the stairs.

Our next surprise came on the second-floor landing, where we were confronted a few moments later by Rebecca Martinez. She was one of the neighbors Cooper had been unable to reach.

The confrontation with my team outside the loft created another dramatic moment. The volatile artist's eyes were red from crying, and she was accusing Lisa Reynolds and Jake of knowing more about Sophia's disappearance than they'd admitted.

"Is it true?" she asked, her voice barely above a whisper. "Is Jake really dead?"

"Excuse me," I said. "Who are you and what's your relationship with Mr. Williams?"

"I'm his neighbor," she replied. "Rebecca Martinez, I live there," she pointed, "at number 4. Jake and I... well, I'm an artist, he's an artist. We... we're friends, I suppose. Is he really dead? Who are you?"

I introduced us both, then looked at her and nodded. "Yes, I'm afraid he is."

And she broke down completely.

She was in her mid-thirties. with short-cropped black hair and paint-stained fingers. She claimed she must have been in the shower when Cooper knocked on her door, and, like Patterson, had heard about his death on the news.

"First Sophia, then Lisa, now Jake," she sobbed. "They're all gone. Everyone Sophia cared about, everyone she worked with, they..." she trailed off then said, "This can't be happening."

"When did you last see Jake?" Corbin asked gently.

"Two, no, three days ago, here on the stairs. I was on my way out. He was on his way in."

"And was there anything different about him?" Corbin asked. "Did he seem happy? Was he in good spirits?"

She frowned, wrinkled her brow, then said, "Now you mention it, he seemed a bit down; nervous, like."

"I'm sorry, but I have to ask you this, Rebecca," he said. "Where were you between ten and eleven last night?"

"In my apartment. Asleep," she replied without hesitation.

"Can anyone verify that?" he asked.

"No! Of course not. I was alone. I'm always alone."

"Well," he said, "if there's anything you can think of that might be helpful, that has my personal cell number." He handed her his card, then looked at me, and we left her standing there staring at his card.

Doc Sheddon arrived around eleven-thirty. He studied the body, his lips pursed, his eyes narrowed, his usual jovial expression absent as he studied Jake's wounds.

"Three stab wounds, all to the chest area to the left of the sternum," he began. "I'd say two penetrated the left ventricle and the third...? Well, I'll know more when I get him to the table. The two wounds to the left ventricle would have caused massive bleeding into the pericardial sac. He died quickly: two to three minutes. Time of death according to the body temperature, between nine-thirty and eleven-thirty. The defensive wounds to the hands are minor by comparison. He fought back, but with little success." He paused for a moment, then said, "Nasty little weapon. I've not seen the like of it before. Some kind of tool, is it?"

I nodded, thinking, trying to picture the scene as it happened. In the end, I just shuddered involuntarily and said, "When will you do the post, Doc?"

"Tomorrow morning, early," he replied. "Will you attend?"

"No," I replied, "but Corbin will."

I turned to Corbin and said, "By the way, I don't see a computer."

"No, Jack arrived just after I did, and he took it away for analysis.."

"I'll call him," I said. "See if he's found anything."

"Jack," I said when he picked up. "D'you have anything for me?"

"Jake Williams' laptop?" he asked. "Sure do. Isn't he supposed to be a sculptor? Would you believe the guy was into canvas preparation and aging techniques? For a sculptor, it looks like he had extensive knowledge of historical art materials and authentication."

"I think he did some of that kind of work for Lisa Reynolds," I replied.

The crime scene processing continued, revealing microscopic evidence that Willis would analyze at the lab—paint samples that didn't match Jake's usual palette and clay residue that seemed to come from much older sources than his contemporary work.

"These trace evidence samples," Willis said, shaking his

head. "I need to have them analyzed, but it looks to me like Jake was working outside his box. Authentication, you say?" He shrugged. "I don't know, Kate."

LATER, back at the department, in my office, we were assembled for our evening briefing. I was seated behind my desk, thinking that Willis's findings raised more questions than answers. I mean, why would a contemporary sculptor be working with historical art materials? And what kind of restoration work required such substantial monthly payments? And why had both victims been so secretive about their business relationships?

"The payments were consistent," Tracy said. *Is she reading my mind?* I wondered.

The rest of my team was seated around the table, while Samson was in his usual place, on his bed under the window.

"Every month, like clockwork, for almost two years," Tracy continued. "That's not how restoration work usually operates. Restorers are usually paid by the job or by the piece."

She was right. Even I knew that. The regularity of the payments suggested an ongoing business relationship rather than individual project work. Whatever Jake was providing to Lisa's gallery, it was valuable enough to justify substantial monthly compensation.

Cooper had been interviewing members of the art community, trying to get an understanding of the authentication practices used in the local galleries. Several artists mentioned rumors about pieces appearing and disappearing from various locations without clear sales records.

"There's been talk," Tony said. "One gallery owner said there was nothing specific, but people in the know were talking about high-value pieces moving through the community without the usual documentation."

The upshot of the meeting was that the evidence was pointing toward something more complex than simple sculpture work. Lisa had been involved in high-value art sales with questionable documentation, Jake had been receiving unusually large payments for unspecified restoration work, and together they'd been generating serious money from activities that were either unknown at that point, or weren't properly recorded.

But someone had discovered whatever it was they were involved in and decided to eliminate them. Whether that someone was a business partner cleaning up loose ends, a defrauded client seeking revenge, or someone else entirely remained to be determined.

As I headed home that evening, I couldn't shake the feeling that we were missing something important. I was now convinced that Jake's death so soon after Lisa's was no coincidence, but I wasn't sure if we were dealing with two simple killings or something more sinister.

And the questions were multiplying faster than the answers. What had Lisa and Jake really been doing together? Why had someone wanted them both dead? And where did the missing student, Sophia Blake, fit into all of this?

By the time I unlocked my front door, I had a nagging suspicion that Jake Williams wouldn't be the last victim, but I couldn't explain why. Maybe it was just cop instinct, or maybe it was the way people in the art community seemed nervous when we asked questions.

I made a mental note to dig deeper into whatever business relationship Lisa and Jake had been hiding. There were obviously secrets in Chattanooga's art world, and people were dying because of them.

I needed answers, and I needed them quickly.

THE MISSING STUDENT

THE MORNING AFTER JAKE WILLIAMS' MURDER, I OFFICIALLY opened an investigation into Sophia Blake's disappearance. Two deaths, a missing student and the now missing Vincent Harper, all in the space of three weeks—Blake had gone missing three weeks earlier—couldn't be coincidental, and the connections between all four victims suggested a pattern rather than random violence.

"Kate," Chief Johnston called as I walked past his office at seven-thirty. "I need a minute, please."

"Just a sec," I said, and went to the break room and tossed what little was left of my coffee and then headed into his office, Samson trailing behind me. The chief was already at his desk, reading what looked like incident reports.

"Close the door," he said without looking up. "Sit down. Tell me about this Blake girl."

I shrugged. "There's not much to tell," I said, settling into the chair in front of his desk. "She's a graduate art student at UTC. She was reported missing three weeks ago. Apparently, she disappeared while investigating authentication practices at local art galleries. Her name keeps coming up in both murder cases."

Johnston finally looked up, his mustache twitching. "Three weeks, you say. That doesn't look good. "

"I agree," I replied. "But I think she's the key to understanding why Lisa Reynolds and Jake Williams were killed. That being so, I've added her to my investigation. As to whether she's alive or dead..." Again, I shrugged. "As you say, it's not looking good."

He leaned back in his chair. "Find her, Kate. This thing's getting bigger by the day, and I need answers before it gets worse."

"Yes, sir."

"And Kate? Keep this quiet. The last thing we need is media speculation about a serial killer targeting the art community."

"I know," I said. "It always amazes me how many of the movers and shakers get antsy when we catch a high-profile case. I guess you can expect a call from the mayor anytime soon."

He gave me a look that would have shriveled a lesser person, then said, "Get out of here, Kate, and keep me informed."

I left his office, spent a few moments in mine, then grabbed Corbin and together with Samson we headed out to UTC to examine Sophia Blake's dormitory room. Fortunately, the university had kept it sealed since her disappearance, initially hoping she'd return, I supposed.

The drive to UTC took me through some of Chattanooga's older neighborhoods, and past the once-proud Victorian houses on Oak Street that had been converted to student housing.

The university's art department on Palmetto Street occupied an entire campus block and felt more like a small town than an academic institution.

I was met by a young woman named Jennifer Walsh, who proclaimed herself to be the resident advisor. "I have the key you requested," she said, "and I'm to accompany you."

I nodded. "Please lead the way."

She was maybe twenty-five, with the earnest demeanor of someone who took her responsibilities seriously. She unlocked the door and stepped aside to let us enter.

The room was on the third floor of a converted Victorian house that served as graduate student housing. The room was small, cluttered, typical of a dedicated student who spent more time studying than housekeeping. Books were stacked everywhere, art supplies scattered across polished wood surfaces, and the walls were covered with reproductions of famous paintings.

But my experience told me this wasn't how Sophia had left it. Personal items were missing, including her laptop. According to Walsh, expensive textbooks and research materials were also missing, but basic clothing and personal effects remained, as if someone had taken only the most valuable and/or incriminating items.

"Have you been in here since Sophia disappeared?" I asked.

"Just to check on things periodically. We keep hoping she'll come back. She was such a dedicated student - it wasn't like her to just disappear."

I nodded, then said to Samson, "What d'you think, Sammy? You want to take a look around?" Out of my periphery, I caught Corbin smiling. I looked at him. He simply winked and then shrugged.

Samson sat for a moment as if contemplating the scene, then rose to his feet and trotted over to the closet, his nose twitching. From there he checked out the bathroom, then returned to the living room, where, in a corner beside the window, he found something. He lay down, his head between his paws.

"What've you got, boy?" I asked as I joined him and dropped to one knee.

He was focused on a specific section of baseboard. I tapped it. He stood, inched closer, his nose twitching. The section sounded hollow. I grabbed the top of it with the fingertips of both hands and pulled. It came away, and in the cavity behind it; I found a thick three-ring binder.

I snapped on a pair of latex gloves, removed the book from the cavity, and flipped through the pages. Basically, it was a notebook full of handwritten research notes. I looked up at Walsh and, holding the book open so she could see it, said, "D'you recognize this handwriting?"

She nodded. "It's Sophia's."

I stood up, took out my phone and called Willis. "Mike, I need you at UTC graduate housing. I think I've found something." I gave him the address and the apartment number, and he said he was on his way.

While waiting for Willis to arrive, I examined Sophia's notes. They were meticulous: detailed observations about specific paintings. She quoted authentication certificates, provenance documentation, and what appeared to be discrepancies in dating.

One name appeared repeatedly: "The Painted Lady - 1847 - Thomas Cole - inconsistent canvas preparation."

The notes were extensive and included photographs in glassine pockets. She'd documented the histories of several paintings and compared them to known examples of authentic work from the same period.

"She was thorough, I'll say that," I muttered as I continued flipping through pages.

"She is," Walsh looked over my shoulder. *Is, not was,* I thought. *Hope springs eternal, I guess.*

"Sophia is always researching something. She spends hours in the library tracking down obscure historical references. Her thesis advisor said she has the most organized research methods he'd ever seen."

I didn't need a warrant to search the place. For one, I had university permission, and for two, I had probable cause in that she'd been missing for three weeks. So, we spent the next thirty minutes until Willis arrived carefully examining the small apartment.

"What've we got?" Willis asked as he entered, his big black case in hand.

"Someone cleaned out this room," I explained. "But they missed these notes hidden behind the baseboard."

Willis began to examine the room, collecting samples from various surfaces and photographing the areas of interest. After maybe ten minutes, he looked up at us and said, "Come on, Kate. You're making me nervous. This is going to take a while, and then I'll need to analyze these samples back at the lab."

I nodded, then said, "But surely you must have an idea of what happened here."

He sighed, rose to his feet, and said, "The dust patterns suggest someone searched this room. That's all I can tell you. Now, get out of here and let me do my job."

"Okay," I said, "but please turn that binder over to Jack when you've finished with it."

We left Willis to his work and returned to my office. As I stepped out of the elevator, I ran into Tony Cooper.

"Captain," he said, "I just finished interviewing Michelle Parry. She lives in the apartment next to Sophia. I thought you should hear what she has to say. Michelle's also a graduate student. She's pretty damn smart. I recorded the interview. You want to listen?"

"My office, Tony. You too, Corbin."

"Now," I said a couple of minutes later as I sat down behind my desk. "Let's hear it."

Tony hit the play button and set his digital recorder down on my desk, then took a seat at the table.

"Sophia was excited about something she'd discovered," Michelle explained. "She'd been researching local painters from the 1800s, trying to authenticate pieces in private collections. She said she'd found something important that people needed to know about."

"What kind of something?" Tony asked.

"She wouldn't say exactly, but she'd been meeting with experts to confirm her findings. She mentioned a painting called 'The Painted Lady.' She said it was culturally significant, but something wasn't right about it."

Michelle continued on to provide additional details about Sophia's research and her habits. "She was incredibly organized," she said. "Everything had to be documented, photographed, and cross-referenced. She kept saying that when you're challenging established authentications, you need bulletproof evidence."

"Did she seem worried about her research?" Tony asked.

"Not worried, exactly. More like... determined."

"What about visitors? Did she have people coming to see her about her research?"

"A few," Michelle continued. "Her thesis advisor, Dr. Patterson, visited occasionally. And there was a woman from the Hunter Museum. Dr. Whitman, I think her name was. They'd discuss technical aspects of authentication."

"Did she seem afraid of anything?" Tony asked.

"No, not that I can remember," Michelle replied. "She

seemed… I dunno, fixated. She did say there were a lot of people who were going to be pissed off by what she'd found."

"Did she mention any strange phone calls…? Or… did you notice any unusual behavior during the days before she disappeared?" Tony asked.

There was a moment of silence, then Michelle continued, "She told me she'd been getting calls from someone she wouldn't identify. She said they were related to her research. And she'd started locking her door, which wasn't like her."

I exchanged glances with Tony across my desk. Anonymous calls and security concerns suggested Sophia had been worried about something or someone.

"Okay, Tony, I get it," I said, rising to my feet. "You can turn that thing off. First, get that call transcribed and make sure I get a copy. Second, I want you to follow up on those phone calls. Check her cell phone records, see if we can identify who was contacting her."

"On it," Tony replied, and he, too, got up, thought for a moment, opened his mouth to speak, changed his mind, said, "On it," again, and left the room.

"Corbin," I said, sitting down again, "I think you and I need to talk to some people about Sophia, starting with her thesis advisor. Let's go."

He frowned and looked pointedly at his watch. "Er, it's almost one-thirty," he said. "Don't you think we should get some lunch?"

He was right; I was hungry too. "It'll have to be McDonald's," I said. "You okay with that?"

"Let's go," he replied, and walked to the door.

"Hey, wait for me," I yelled as I stood up and grabbed my things.

FORTY-FIVE MINUTES later we arrived at the university's art department, where we were met by the department secretary, a rather officious—and wary—lady in her mid-forties by the name of Renee Maxwell. She became more cooperative once I explained we were treating Sophia's disappearance as a potential homicide.

"Her thesis advisor is Professor Patterson," Maxwell explained, checking her records. "Sophia was researching 19th-century painters of the Tri-state area, and the authentication practices of local galleries."

Maxwell also provided additional details about Sophia's academic standing. "She's a brilliant student. She maintained a 4.0 GPA and published undergraduate research. Her professors all describe her as exceptionally gifted and meticulous about her documentation."

That matched what we'd already learned - Sophia had developed considerable expertise in canvas dating and paint analysis, skills that would make her dangerous to anyone involved in art fraud.

PROFESSOR PATTERSON'S office was in the art building, a cramped space filled with books, chemicals, and microscopy equipment. The walls were covered with charts showing paint composition and aging patterns.

Patterson looked worse than he had at Jake's crime scene. His hands shook as he poured coffee, and his eyes were red-rimmed with exhaustion.

"Sophia was brilliant," he said, his voice breaking slightly. "She had an intuitive understanding of historical art techniques I've rarely seen in graduate students. Her thesis was a groundbreaking work on local art authentication."

"What specifically was she investigating?" I asked.

"She claimed she'd identified several paintings in local collections that had questionable provenance," he replied. "Her research suggested some pieces weren't what they claimed to be."

"Professor," I said, "if you would, please walk me through Sophia's research process."

"She'd start with a cursory physical examination of the piece and from there she would proceed to historical documentation - sales records, exhibition catalogs, insurance appraisals. Then she'd examine the artwork in depth, looking for inconsistencies in materials or techniques. Finally, she'd use chemical analysis to verify age and authenticity."

"What kind of inconsistencies specifically?" Corbin asked. I looked at him in surprise. He merely shrugged.

"Paint composition that didn't match the historical period," Patterson replied. "Canvas preparation techniques that weren't used until decades later, aging patterns that appeared artificial rather than natural."

"Professor, I need to ask you about your relationship with Jake Williams," I said.

Patterson's reaction was immediate. He knocked over his coffee cup, sending liquid across his desk. "I told you yesterday," he said, "we consulted occasionally on authentication questions. Jake had developed some techniques that were useful for dating questionable pieces."

"What techniques?" Corbin asked.

"Aging methods. Canvas preparation. Jake understood how to make new materials look old, which helped us identify when someone was trying to pass off a recent work as historical."

That was an interesting skill set for someone to possess. Understanding how to age materials artificially could just as easily be used to create convincing forgeries.

"That wasn't Jake's purview, was it, Professor?" I asked. "How did Jake come to develop such techniques?"

"He said he'd learned them from another restorer, someone who specialized in historical preservation. He was always secretive about his methods; claimed they were trade secrets."

"Did Sophia work directly with Jake?" I asked.

"A few times. She'd bring him samples for analysis, and he'd help her understand the aging processes. But lately, she'd been questioning some of his conclusions."

"Oh yes? What kind of questions?" Corbin asked.

Patterson turned to look at him, hesitated for a moment, then said. "She thought some of his aging techniques seemed a little too good, but she didn't elaborate on it. "

"Where's Sophia, Professor?" I asked directly.

"I DON'T KNOW!" he shouted, then immediately lowered his voice. "I'm sorry. I've been under a lot of stress lately. If I knew where she was, don't you think I'd tell you?"

Maybe. Maybe not. I thought, watching his eyes.

"Professor," I said quietly, "I need you to provide me with a complete list of everyone Sophia was working with, especially those concerning her research. Names, contact information, and the nature of their involvement."

"Of course. I'll have it ready for you tomorrow."

WE LEFT Patterson's office with more questions than answers and headed to the Hunter Museum of American Art to interview Dr. Whitman. By then it was mid-afternoon and the museum was quiet, perfect for an in-depth conversation.

Dr. Whitman met us in her lab, a fascinating blend of cutting-edge technology and traditional craftsmanship. She seemed genuinely pleased to see us.

"Captain Gazzara, and you've brought your dog. How nice. So how can I help you today?"

"I want to talk to you about Sophia Blake," I said. "I understand you were working with her on her thesis research."

Dr. Whitman frowned slightly. "Yes, Sophia consulted with me occasionally. She was a graduate student in need of expert guidance."

"What kind of guidance?" Corbin asked. Again, I glanced at him. This time I got no reaction from him.

"Specifically, technical information about canvas dating, paint analysis, historical painting techniques. The specialized knowledge that takes years to develop."

I nodded as I looked around her laboratory. It was impressive, well organized and filled with expensive equipment, including a scanning electron microscope, chemical testing apparatus, and digital imaging systems that could reveal layers of paint invisible to the naked eye.

"What exactly do you do here, Dr. Whitman?" I asked.

"I restore paintings," she replied simply.

"And all this equipment?" I asked.

She smiled. "It would take years to fully explain what I do here. Put simply, we can determine the age of paint layers, identify historical pigments, and even date canvas materials based on fiber composition and weaving patterns. It's quite remarkable what modern technology can reveal about historical artwork."

Samson seemed completely at home with Dr. Whitman, even falling asleep at her feet during our conversation.

"Dr. Whitman, what can you tell me about a painting called 'The Painted Lady'?"

She stared at me for a moment, then said, "How d'you know about that, Captain?"

"It came up during the course of our investigation," I replied.

She nodded, took a deep breath, then said, "It's a Thomas Cole piece from 1847, one of only three known works he created during his visit to Chattanooga. It's culturally significant because it documents the artistic sophistication that existed here before the Civil War."

"Was Sophia researching this painting?" I asked, already knowing the answer.

"She was," she replied. "And she had concerns about its authenticity. She claimed the provenance appeared questionable, and some of the technical aspects didn't match what we'd expect from Cole's work."

"Any specific concerns?" Corbin asked.

"She claimed she was certain the canvas preparation didn't match Cole's typical methods. The pigment composition included materials that weren't commonly available in 1847. And the aging seemed... artificial."

"Did you see the painting?" Corbin asked. "What did you tell her?"

"Yes, of course. I've seen the painting many times. I encouraged her to document her findings carefully. If a piece of that significance was questionable, it needed to be investigated properly."

"What was your opinion, Doctor?" I asked. "Is it authentic, or is it a fake?"

She appeared shocked by the question. "The answer to that is beyond my area of expertise," she replied. "I don't evaluate artwork, I restore it."

"But you're an expert, Doctor," I said.

"True, but as I said, authentication is not my area of expertise, and I have to be careful about offering opinions about significant works of art, even to you, Captain."

Whitman's knowledge of art authentication and her

connection to Sophia's research made her a valuable witness. But, like everyone in this case, she seemed to be hiding something.

"Who currently owns 'The Painted Lady'?" I asked.

"It's in a private collection," she replied. "Marcus Webb purchased it about two years ago through Lisa Reynolds' gallery. He paid quite a substantial sum for it."

Marcus Webb again. The same collector who'd been demanding refunds from Reynolds for what he claimed were fraudulent pieces.

"When did you last see Sophia?" I asked.

"About a month ago. She came to the museum to discuss her findings. She was excited about her research but also concerned about the implications."

"What implications?" I asked.

"If 'The Painted Lady' was a forgery, it would raise questions about other pieces in local collections. The financial and cultural impact could be enormous."

As usual, I left the interview with more questions than answers. Dr. Whitman's cooperation was helpful, but I needed to understand the broader academic context of Sophia's research. Who else knew about her work? Were there professional rivalries that might have put her in danger? And, most importantly, who benefited from her death, if she was indeed dead.

Back at my office, I called the UTC art department to get a better understanding of the academic community surrounding Sophia's thesis work. This time the department secretary, Renee Maxwell, again seemed eager to cooperate.

"Well," she said conspiratorially, "Professor Patterson has had some conflicts with other researchers," she explained. "There's a lot of competition for grants, publication opportunities, and recognition. Dr. Angela Foster at Chattanooga State has been particularly critical of his methods."

"Really?" I said. "What kind of criticism?"

"She questioned his techniques and accused him of being too willing to challenge established attributions. There was a heated exchange at a conference last year about proper research methodology."

I smiled to myself. It sounded to me like the kind of professional rivalry that goes on everywhere, but it could affect a graduate student's career prospects. Angela Foster, an art history professor at Chattanooga State, had been competing with Patterson for research grants and had publicly criticized Sophia's thesis.

I thanked the secretary for her time and hung up. Then, after several moments of thought, I decided to pay Dr. Foster a visit, but not until tomorrow.

ARTS AND CRAFTS

AFTER A RESTLESS NIGHT, I ROSE EARLY AND WENT FOR A short run. Then I made Sammy and me a little breakfast of scrambled eggs for me and his favorite kibbles for him. By eight-thirty, I was in my office tidying some outstanding paperwork. That done, I refilled my to-go cup, and we headed out.

Chattanooga State's art building on Amnicola Highway was smaller than UTC's, but Foster's office was easy to find. She was a woman in her fifties with mousy hair that was badly in need of styling, sharp eyes and an air of professional skepticism. When I explained I was investigating Sophia Blake's disappearance, her reaction was... best described as dismissive.

"Patterson's student was out of her depth," Foster declared. "Authentication requires years of experience, not just graduate-level enthusiasm. Her conclusions about local paintings were preliminary at best."

Foster's office was smaller than Patterson's but equally cluttered with research materials. She, too, specialized in

American art from the 19th century, making her more than qualified to evaluate Sophia's work.

"What specifically did you disagree with in Sophia's research?" I asked.

"Her methodology was sound, but her conclusions were too definitive. She was making accusations about established pieces without sufficient evidence to support her claims."

Foster's professional jealousy provided a motive for harming Patterson's reputation through his student. But her academic credentials also gave her the expertise to recognize art fraud.

"Did you know Jake Williams?" I asked.

"I'd heard of him. He was a local sculptor who did some restoration work. I believe Patterson consulted with him occasionally on technical matters."

"What did you think of his work?" I asked.

"Competent, but nothing special. I never understood why Patterson relied on him so heavily."

"Professor Foster, do you have access to art authentication equipment?"

"Limited access. We have some basic analysis tools, but nothing like the sophisticated equipment at the Hunter Museum."

"Did you ever meet with Sophia Blake personally about her research?"

Foster's expression hardened. "She contacted me once, asking for my opinion on her methodology. I told her the same thing I'm telling you, that she was making accusations without sufficient evidence."

"What kind of accusations?" I asked.

"She claimed that several established pieces in local collections were questionable. That's a serious charge that could damage reputations and destroy market confidence. You don't make those kinds of claims lightly."

"Did she seem afraid when you spoke with her?"

"Afraid? No, naïve and overconfident? Yes. She thought her limited graduate training qualified her to challenge experts with decades of experience."

I could see that this interview wasn't going to yield much more useful information. Foster's professional jealousy was obvious, but her disdain seemed genuine rather than calculated, so I closed the interview.

"Professor, if you think of anything else that might be helpful, please call me," I said, handing her my card.

After leaving Foster's office, I decided to follow up on another angle. Father Michael Blake had been mentioned during our initial investigation as someone who worked with young artists. His youth program had placed kids in various galleries, including Lisa's.

St. Francis Church was in an older section of downtown, a modest brick building with stained glass windows that cast colorful patterns across the worn wooden pews. I found Father Blake in his office behind the sanctuary; a small room filled with art supplies and photographs of young people displaying their work.

He was in his sixties, with graying hair and kind eyes. When I explained I was investigating Sophia Blake's disappearance, he immediately set aside his paperwork and gave me his full attention.

"These kids come from difficult backgrounds," Father Blake explained, gesturing to the photographs on his wall. "Some are aging out of foster care; others are from broken homes. Art gives them hope, a way to express themselves and maybe build a future."

He stood up and walked to a display case filled with pottery, paintings, and small sculptures. "We provide supplies, workspace, and, most importantly, connections to the professional art community. I've placed over thirty young people in part-time positions at local galleries and studios over the past five years."

"What kind of work do they do?" I asked.

"Basic tasks, mostly cleaning, moving artwork, helping with installations. But it gives them exposure to the business side of art and helps them understand how art galleries operate."

Blake obviously had genuine concern for his students. They weren't just statistics to him; they were young people he'd invested in personally.

"These kids are vulnerable," he said. "They're passionate about art but naïve about business practices. I'd hate to think someone was exploiting that passion for illegal purposes."

"Did any of them know Sophia Blake?" I asked.

"Know?" He frowned, staring at one of the small sculptures. "I don't think any of them really knew her, though a couple of them mentioned her. She'd visited some of the galleries where they worked, asking questions. The kids liked her. They said she was genuinely interested in their work."

"What kind of questions was she asking?" I said.

"She wanted to know how galleries determined the authenticity of pieces, who provided authentication certificates, and whether anyone had ever questioned the provenance of expensive artwork."

Samson nudged his hand with his nose. He looked down and smiled. "All God's creatures," he muttered as he fondled the dog's ears. Then he looked up at me and said, "What a beautiful dog, Captain."

"Thank you, Father. He obviously likes you." He nodded absently, and I said, "Can we talk for a minute about Lisa Reynolds' gallery? Did any of your students work there, and did any of them mention unusual activities there?"

"Nothing specific, but some felt uncomfortable with certain aspects of the work. Late-night activities, pieces that appeared one night and disappeared the next. I told them to focus on their art and not worry about business matters."

"Did they mention Sophia visiting the gallery?"

"Yes, several times. I understand she was asking very detailed questions about some specific pieces, taking photographs, and making notes. I was also told that Lisa seemed uncomfortable with her visits."

I spent another few minutes with Father Blake, getting more details about his students' experiences at various galleries. And the more I learned about Sophia, the clearer it became that she'd been conducting a systematic investigation into irregularities, specifically at the Reynolds gallery.

"One last question, Father," I said. "From what you know of Sophia, did she seem worried about anything?"

He slowly shook his head. "As I said, I didn't know her that well," he replied. "But no, not during the few times I met her, but I could tell she was a determined young woman. She had an intensity about her. I don't think I ever saw her smile."

I thanked Father Blake for his time and headed back to the police department, where I found Jack hunched over his computer screens in the computer forensics lab. He'd been analyzing Sophia's phone records, social media, and the binder we'd recovered from her apartment. His workspace was cluttered with printouts, notes, and multiple monitors displaying various aspects of Sophia's digital life.

"What've you got for me, Jack?" I asked, pulling up a chair beside his desk.

"Interesting stuff," he replied, not looking up from his monitors. "She was methodical; I'll give her that. The binder contains detailed notes about paintings, lots of photographs and cross-referenced documentation."

"What kind of documentation?" I asked, leaning forward,

my elbows on my knees, my hands clasped together in front of me.

"Authentication certificates mostly, sales records, insurance appraisals. She was tracking several specific pieces and their histories. But here's the thing: she was asking a lot of questions about where these pieces came from."

Jack showed me screenshots of Sophia's research files. The organization was impressive: folders sorted by gallery, by time period, by artist. Each entry included photographs, documentation, and detailed notes about authentication concerns.

"She was particularly interested in pieces from the 1800s," Jack continued. "Local artists, historical significance, that kind of thing. And she kept notes of discrepancies in the paperwork."

"Discrepancies?" I asked, frowning. "What kind of discrepancies?"

"Gaps in ownership history, authentication certificates that couldn't be verified, pieces that appeared on the market without clear provenance. Nothing illegal necessarily, but enough to raise questions."

"D'you know how long she'd been working on it?"

"Based on the dates of these notes, over a year," he replied. "This wasn't casual research she was doing. She was building a comprehensive database of questionable pieces."

Jack showed me more of the handwritten notes we'd found in Sophia's room. Museum curators, university professors, independent appraisers; it seemed she'd been consulting with anyone who might help verify her findings.

"There's more," Jack continued, pointing to phone records we'd obtained. "She'd been getting calls from someone using a burner phone. Regular contact over the past month, including a call the day before she disappeared."

"Any way to trace the burner?" I asked.

He glanced at me, then said, "You know better than that, Kate. It's unlikely. Used to be they all came from Walmart. Now there are several hundred outlets in Chattanooga alone, never mind Hamilton County, but I'm working on it."

"What about her regular phone contacts?"

"According to her texts, she was supposed to meet with someone the day after she disappeared. The meeting location was texted to her from the same burner number."

I left Jack to continue his digital investigation and decided to follow up with some of the other people who'd been mentioned during our inquiry. The art community in Chattanooga was small enough that everyone seemed connected to everyone else. Some of them were even mentioned in Sophia's notes. One in particular was Grace Parker, the blogger who'd also been tracking questionable practices. Her blog had gained attention for its investigative approach to art market issues, and I figured she might have insights into what Sophia had been researching.

That afternoon, late, at around four, I drove back to the arts district to meet with Grace Parker.

I found Grace in a coffee shop near the Reynolds Gallery, working on her laptop surrounded by notebooks and printed articles. She was a skinny woman in her late twenties, with brown hair and the intense focus of someone passionate about her work.

"Captain Gazzara?" she said. "Hello again. I've been following your investigation in the news. This is connected to the Lisa Reynolds investigation, isn't it?"

"You have?" I asked. "How so?"

"Because I've been tracking similar issues nationwide for my blog. Galleries that can't provide adequate documentation for high-value pieces, authentication certificates that raise questions, buyers who discover problems with their purchases months after the sale."

Grace's perspective as a journalist had given her a different angle on the same problems Sophia had been researching. Her blog posts revealed a pattern of concerns that extended way beyond any single gallery.

"How did you first become aware of these issues?" I asked.

"Tips from readers mostly," she replied. "People who'd purchased artwork and later had questions about authenticity. It was one in particular in New York that triggered my investigation, and when this thing at the Reynolds gallery came up... Well, as you can imagine, it caught my attention. Any tidbits you can share with me, Captain?"

I smiled at her and ignored the question. "Tell me what you found," I said.

"Here in Chattanooga?" she asked. "Not much. Nationwide? Pieces appearing on the market with impressive documentation, but when buyers tried to verify the details, they'd hit dead ends. Previous owners who couldn't be contacted, auction houses with incomplete records, that sort of thing."

Grace showed me printouts of her blog posts, each documenting specific cases of authentication problems. The financial amounts were significant: individual pieces worth tens of thousands of dollars, with questions about their legitimacy.

"Did you know Sophia Blake?" I asked.

She shrugged and made a face. "Not really. We'd been in contact by email. She was interested in my blog posts. We were supposed to meet to discuss her research."

"When was this meeting supposed to happen?"

"The day after she disappeared. She said she had evidence that would support some of my blog posts."

Another person who was supposed to meet with Sophia the day after she vanished. The timing couldn't be coincidental.

"Did she mention what that evidence was?" I asked.

"No, she didn't say specifically, but she mentioned having documentation about some pieces with questionable provenance. She seemed excited about what she'd discovered."

I decided there wasn't anything more I could learn from her, so I thanked her for her time and took my leave.

Before heading back to the department, though, I decided to stop by Carmen Rodriguez's insurance office. My thought was that her investigation into art-related claims might provide additional context for what Sophia had been researching. The insurance angle could reveal the financial scope of any problems in the local art market.

Carmen worked out of a small office in a downtown insurance building. She was in her early forties with prematurely graying hair and the methodical demeanor of someone who'd spent years in a boring and difficult profession. She'd been handling art insurance cases for several years, as evidenced by her desk covered with claim files and reports.

"Ms. Rodriguez? I'm Captain Gazzara, Chattanooga Police. We met at the Reynolds Gallery. I'm investigating the disappearance of Sophia Blake and the recent murders of Lisa Reynolds and Jake Williams. I understand you've been handling art insurance claims that might be related to Reynolds and Williams."

"Really?" she asked dryly. "Yes, of course I remember you, but I'm not sure how I can be of help, but if I can, I will. So first, let me say this: Yes, I've been seeing more disputes lately," she said, pulling out a thick file folder. "It goes like this: a buyer purchases a painting, then months later orders an independent appraisal." She paused for a moment, then continued, "And that appraisal raises questions about the painting's authenticity. It's a pattern that's been developing over the past two years," she said, showing me a stack of about a half-dozen claim files. "Buyers purchase expensive artwork, then later discover there's a problem. The financial implications are significant."

I looked at the claims in her hand. "That's got to be expensive," I said.

"You betcha," she said. "These seven individual claims total over six hundred thousand dollars. If there is a systematic problem with authentication, the potential liability could be enormous."

Carmen walked me through several of the case files, explaining the typical progression of events. Initial purchase with impressive documentation, later questions about authenticity, disputes between buyers and sellers, and insurance claims when pieces were proved to have been misrepresented.

"What's concerning is the consistency of the pattern," she continued. "Similar documentation problems, similar types of pieces, similar gaps in provenance. It suggests more than random authentication errors."

"Are you seeing this pattern in other cities?"

"Some, but Chattanooga has had an unusual concentration of these cases, all centered on the Reynolds Gallery. Given the size of our art market, and that gallery in particular, the number of problematic pieces is disproportionately high."

"Any theories about why that might be?" I asked.

"Well, I suppose it could be coincidence, or it could be something more serious. That's why I've been documenting everything carefully."

As I drove back to the department, I couldn't help but think about Sophia Blake, a young graduate student, obviously dedicated to her cause, asking the right questions about something that was making a lot of people nervous. Her research had identified serious problems with the way someone was authenticating pieces of what appeared to be significant art. She'd been making waves. Whether she'd uncovered a few simple business irregularities or something more serious remained to be determined. But one thing was obvious to me: her questions had made someone angry enough to kill her. *But why kill Lisa Reynolds and Jake Williams...? Sophia? Yes, that I could understand. But the others? And then there was Vincent Harper. What about him?* I wondered.

Tomorrow, I decided I'd start connecting the dots between Sophia's research and the murders of Lisa Reynolds and Jake Williams. It was clear that someone was eliminating people who knew too much about irregularities in the art market, and we needed to identify them before they struck again.

One thing I was certain of was that the missing student held the key to understanding what was really happening in Chattanooga's art world, but whether we'd find her alive or dead remained to be seen.

5

CANVAS AND DECEPTION

THE DISCOVERY OF WHAT LISA REYNOLDS AND JAKE WILLIAMS had really been doing came about through a combination of dogged police work and pure dumb luck. It was Tracy who finally made the connection two days after my interviews with the art community, while she was going through Jake's financial records for the third time.

"Kate," she called from her desk phone in the situation room. "I think I've found something. Can you come?"

I was in my office, going over a stack of reports. It was mid-morning, and the situation room was buzzing with the usual activity: phones ringing, detectives typing reports, the coffee maker gurgling in the corner. Through my office window, I could see Tracy had that look: the one she gets when she's found something important but isn't quite sure what it means yet.

"What've you got?" I asked.

"Jake Williams had a storage unit," she said, waving what looked like a bank statement over her head. "Monthly payments for the past two years. The address is way out on Ringgold Road."

I pushed back from my desk and walked over to look at the statement. "A storage unit, huh? Talk to me, Tracy."

"The payments started right around the time he began receiving those large monthly checks from Lisa's gallery."

Corbin looked up from his own paperwork, a half-eaten sandwich forgotten on his desk. "Could be where he kept his supplies," he said.

"Could be," I said. "How much was he paying?"

"Two hundred fifty dollars a month," Tracy replied. "That's a pretty big unit for just storing art supplies."

"Tracy, get a warrant and then meet us at the unit. Use Judge Strange and tell him I asked for it to be expedited." I paused, thought for a minute, then said, "I want to see what Jake Williams thought was worth hiding in a high-dollar storage facility. Corbin, don't go anywhere. Tracy, call me when you have the warrant."

While Tracy worked on the warrant, I called Willis to give him a heads up. "Mike, we might have something. Jake Williams had a storage unit. We're going to take a look. It could be important."

"You want me to stand by?" he asked.

"Yes, but let me take a look first. It could be nothing. If it is, no harm, no foul. But I'm hoping..." I trailed off. There was no need to say more. He knew what I was talking about.

Three hours later, we were standing outside the U-Store-It facility on Ringgold Road, watching the manager fumble with a large ring of keys. The place looked like every other storage facility I'd ever seen: rows of identical metal buildings with overhead doors, designed for people who had more stuff than space.

"Unit 47B," the manager, Earl, said. He was a thin man in his sixties with a wispy beard who seemed nervous about having police on his property. "Williams paid up through the next three months. Real particular about his privacy, that one. Never saw him here during regular hours."

"What do you mean?" I asked.

"He always came late at night or real early in the morning. Paid in cash, never wanted to chat. Some tenants, they're friendly, you know? Williams, not so much. He just wanted to do his business and leave."

That was interesting. If Jake had been using this place for legitimate restoration work, why the secrecy?

Earl led us down a gravel road between the storage buildings. The facility was larger than it looked from the street, with maybe two hundred units spread across several acres. Unit 47B was in the back row, away from the main office and the busier sections.

"Here we go," Earl said, inserting a key into the padlock. "You want me to stay, or...?"

"We'll take it from here," I said. "Thanks for your cooperation."

Earl nodded and headed back toward his office, clearly relieved to be away from whatever police business was about to unfold.

I lifted the overhead door, and what we found inside stopped me cold.

The storage unit—it was the size of a small warehouse—had been converted into a sophisticated workshop. Tables lined with art supplies, chemical baths, specialized equipment for paint removal, and something that looked like a professional drying system. But what really caught my attention were the paintings.

"Oh my," Corbin muttered, his voice barely above a whisper.

Dozens of them, in various stages of what could only be described as destruction. Old paintings that had been partially stripped, their original artwork scraped away to reveal the bare canvas beneath. Paint chips and canvas fragments littered the floor like the remains of a cultural massacre.

The smell hit me next: a combination of chemical solvents, old paint, and something else I couldn't identify. Whatever it was, it was the smell of destruction.

I took out my phone and tapped my speed dial. "Mike," I said when Willis picked up. "I need you at the U-Store-It on Ringgold Road. Bring your full team and a lot of evidence bags. We've got a major crime scene here."

"What kind of crime scene? Someone dead?"

"The kind that's going to make you sick to your stomach," I replied caustically.

While waiting for Willis, I walked carefully through the unit, trying not to disturb anything. Samson stayed close beside me, his nose quivering. It was as if even he could sense that something terrible had happened in this place.

The setup was sophisticated. Professional-grade equipment, chemical baths with proper ventilation, even a climate control system to maintain optimal conditions for the work being done. Someone had invested serious money in this operation.

On one workbench, I found what appeared to be the remains of what once had been a painting. Only fragments of the image remained around the edges, but it was enough to see that it had once been a significant piece of artwork. The technique was obvious: strip away the original painting, leave the artist's notes intact on the back, then use the canvas as the foundation for a forgery of the original image that would pass scientific dating tests. Why would they do that, forge an original painting? We were soon to find out that Lisa and Jake were buying up damaged pieces for a fraction of what they would have been worth in pristine condition: water damaged, fire damaged, mold. There had been plenty of them recovered from Germany, Poland, France and other Nazi-occupied countries by the Monument Men.

"Hey, come and look at this," Tracy called from the back of the unit.

She was standing beside a filing cabinet filled with documentation. Photographs of original paintings before they were destroyed, records of which pieces had been acquired and how they'd been processed, even sales records for the finished forgeries.

"He kept records of everything," she said, flipping through folders. "Like they were running a legitimate business."

I joined her at the filing cabinet and started looking through the files with her. The organization was meticulous. Each destroyed painting had its own folder with before and after photographs, acquisition records, processing notes, and sales documentation for the forgery created from its canvas.

"Tracy, look at these acquisition records. Most of these pieces came from museums, but some came from estate sales, others from private collections, all of them described as 'damaged' artwork."

"And look at these prices," she replied, pointing to purchase records. "They were buying paintings that were supposedly too damaged to restore for a few thousand dollars. Then they stripped them to the canvas to create forgeries of the originals worth hundreds of thousands. It's genius."

"Genius or not, it's still fraud," I muttered.

"Of course—" Tracy began, but I cut her off.

"Wait a minute," I said. "We're missing something obvious here. Who painted these forgeries? Jake was a sculptor. Lisa owned a gallery. Neither of them had the artistic skill to create convincing paintings in the style of Cole or any of these other masters."

Corbin, who was now standing beside me, nodded.

"You're right. These aren't amateur copies. They had to fool experts and pass scientific analysis."

"Exactly," I muttered thoughtfully. "It has to be someone with serious artistic talent and deep knowledge of 19th-century painting techniques who created these forgeries. That level of skill takes years to develop."

"So we've got another player in this network," Tracy said, looking around the storage unit. "Someone we haven't identified yet."

"Well," Corbin said, "we know it couldn't have been Jake or Lisa, but they must have known who it was. "

Yeah," Tracy said. "You don't get to this level of skill watching The Joy of Painting."

"And if our killer is systematically eliminating everyone connected to the forgery operation," I continued, "the forger could be the next target."

"Or they could already be dead," Corbin observed grimly.

"Either way, we need to find them. Fast," I muttered.

Willis arrived twenty minutes later with his full forensics team, and his reaction was immediate and visceral. "Damn," he said, surveying the damage. "This is... barbaric."

Barbaric? I thought. *It was barbaric how they became damaged in the first place. But the damage was already done. That someone had used them to recreate the originals and then sell them as the originals. That was...*

I turned to Willis and said, "I need you to take this place apart. I want to know everything: how long this has been going on, how many pieces they destroyed, who else was involved, and most importantly, who the hell was skilled enough to paint these forgeries? It wasn't Jake, and it wasn't Lisa. Someone else did this work, and we need to find them now, before our killer does. Got it?"

Willis glared at me, and I knew I'd stepped over the line. "Well, Kate," he said, "if there's one thing I learned during my more than twenty-seven years doing this job, it's that you can't rush it. I can't wave a magic wand and make evidence appear out of thin air; this is going to take time. Real forensic work, not TV bullshit. But yeah, I'll take this place apart molecule by molecule if that's what it takes. Just don't expect miracles by dinnertime."

I reached out, put my hand on his shoulder and said, "Of course. I'm sorry, Mike. It's just that—"

"Yeah, I know," he said dryly. "It's frustrating, but ain't it always?" He paused for a moment, then smiled up at me, nodded, and turned away to direct his team to photograph everything before they started collecting evidence. I shook my head. The scope of the operation was staggering - this had been going on for years.

It wasn't ten minutes later when he called me from a corner of the unit. "Kate, d'you have a minute?"

"You're not going to like this," he said. He was standing beside a partially destroyed painting. It was larger than most of the others. Most of the original artwork had been stripped away, but I could still see fragments of what had once been a landscape scene. The craftsmanship that remained was exquisite. I was looking at what once had been a masterpiece.

"Now look at these," Willis said, pointing to perhaps twenty small brass plaques that someone, presumably Jake Williams, had laid out in two rows on top of the workbench.

"Geez," I said as I picked one of them up, "Mrs. Dana Louise Wilkins - John Singer Sargent - 1897."

I stared at it. Even I had heard of Sargent. What I was looking at was the remains of a culturally significant piece. I learned later that Sargent's original oils were selling for upward of $30,000, with some in the millions of dollars.

I replaced the plaque and turned again to the remains of the painting. "Sons of bitches," I muttered, staring at the pathetic remains of what had once been a priceless work of art.

"And there are more over there," Willis said, pointing to another, smaller bench next to the one we were looking at.

"How many, Mike?" I asked.

"Based on what I can see so far, maybe forty or fifty pieces. I don't think any of them were masterpieces other than the Sargent piece. But the total value of the originals they destroyed? Probably close to a million dollars."

Willis's team worked on documenting and collecting evidence. Slowly but surely, the contents of the storage unit revealed the full scope of Lisa and Jake's operation. They'd been purchasing old, damaged paintings at bargain prices, stripping away the original paintwork, and using the 18th and 19th century canvases to create sophisticated forgeries. The genius, as Tracy had called it, was in the canvas, complete in many cases with the original notes by the artist. Only an expert conducting a scientific examination of the painting technique and style would spot the fraud, which is exactly what Sophia Blake was doing.

"The process was sophisticated," Willis explained as his team worked. "They'd photograph the original piece, then systematically remove all the paint using chemical solvents. The aged canvas would then be used as the foundation for a new painting of the original or maybe even a new painting in the style of whatever artist they wanted to forge."

"How long would this process take?" I asked.

"For each piece?" he paused for a second, frowning, then said, "Probably weeks. Months, maybe. The paint removal alone would take days to do properly without damaging the canvas. Then they'd need time to create the new artwork and age it appropriately."

As the evidence collection continued, I stood back, leaning against the doorframe, my arms crossed over my chest, watching, thinking, what had been happening here was fraud on a grand scale.

Meanwhile, Corbin was outside at the open hatch of my SUV, examining purchase records from the filing cabinet. "Kate, come and look at this. They were buying pieces from all over, even as far away as Budapest. Estate sales, private collectors, even museums disposing of 'damaged' works." He made finger quotes around the word damaged.

"Museums?" I asked as I joined him.

"Yep, look," he said as I leaned over his shoulder. "Here's a receipt from the Alana Taggart Museum in Atlanta for 'A fire-damaged landscape, artist unknown, but attributed to the Hudson River School, purchased for conservation study.'" He looked at me and, frowning, repeated, "Conservation study?"

"They were lying to museums about their intention?" I said.

"Apparently," Corbin replied.

"Okay," I said. "I've seen enough. Box that stuff up, and I'll sign for it. Let's go back to the office."

Then I went looking for Tracy and told her the same thing, and that we were to meet back in the office in an hour. I then told Mike where I'd be if he needed me.

Back in my office, after stopping by the Hardee's drive-through to grab an on-the-go late lunch, we spread out the evidence on the big round table and tried to make sense of the scope of the crime. Jack North began to go through the purchase records we'd found in the storage unit file cabinet, while Tracy worked through the financial documentation, bank records and such.

I sat back in my chair, my fingers linked behind my neck, staring at the pile of paper on the table, and wondering what the hell I'd gotten myself into. I wasn't an art detective. I was homicide. And yes, that's what I had, two deaths for sure and perhaps a third, and maybe even a fourth, but the implications of what we were looking at were staggering.

I leaned forward, rubbed my hands together, and said, "It's time I talked to the chief."

Five minutes later, I was in his outer office talking to Christy, his PA.

"Can I see him?" I asked, both my hands on her desktop.

She picked up her desk phone and tapped a button. "Captain Gazzara's here to see you."

She listened for a moment, hung up, then looked up and said, "You can go on in. He's in a good mood. Please don't spoil it."

I knocked and entered his office. The big man was behind his desk, reading what looked like budget reports. He looked up as I entered.

"Kate. What can I do for you?"

"Well," I said, taking a seat in front of his desk. "I... The Lisa Reynolds case. It's taken a bit of a turn, and I thought I should run it by you. It goes way deeper than just a simple homicide case."

He leaned back in his chair, both hands on top of his desk, and stared at me. "Go on," he said eventually.

"We know what they were up to, Chief," I said. "We found a storage unit out on Ringgold Road. It looks like we've stumbled onto a major art fraud operation. They were reworking 'damaged' artwork, creating forgeries." This time it was me that made finger quotes around the word damaged.

He nodded slowly, then said, "Go on."

"What they were doing was buying damaged historical paintings at bargain prices, then stripping away the original artwork to use the aged canvas to create forgeries."

Johnston's expression grew grim as I explained the process. "Show me," he said.

I pulled up the photographs I'd taken with my phone and handed it to him.

He flipped slowly through them, then looked at me and said, "This is terrible. How many pieces are we talking about?"

"According to Willis... could be as many as fifty over the past two years. Including The Painted Lady, the Thomas Cole piece that Marcus Webb paid three-hundred thousand for."

"The media's going to have a field day with this," Johnston said, handing back my phone.

"It gets worse," I continued. "From what we've learned so far, it seems some of these pieces were donated to museums by families who thought they were preserving cultural heritage. Instead, they ended up being sold as damaged goods. One was donated by an Atlanta museum for restorative research, or something like that."

Johnston stood up, walked to his window, and looked out. "D'you think any of the museums were involved in the fraud, Kate?"

"No, not deliberately," I replied, "but they were deceived. I believe Lisa and Jake presented themselves as legitimate conservators interested in studying damaged pieces for research purposes. The museums thought they were contributing to art preservation."

"How many museums?"

"We're still checking, but the records show acquisitions from at least three institutions in the Southeast. Probably more. Even two in Paris, France, and one in London."

"So how do we handle the public relations aspect?" he asked, turning away from the window.

That wasn't a question I would have expected, but I answered it. "Carefully," I said. "We need to protect the legitimate museums and galleries that were deceived. And Chief? We still don't know who painted the forgeries."

Johnston sat back down heavily, looked at me and sighed. "And you have no leads?"

I shook my head. "No, none, but we're working on it. We think it's possible the forger could be the next target."

"Keep me informed, Captain," he said as he picked up one of his reports.

And so, I was dismissed.

SOMETIME AROUND MID-AFTERNOON, considering our new understanding of what had been done to his paintings, I decided to go talk again to Marcus Webb. I figured the wealthy collector deserved to know the full extent of the fraud he'd unknowingly took part in. I wasn't happy about it. It was a situation something akin to having to tell a family member that their loved one had been murdered, which in his case was probably true. After all, someone had murdered his paintings, and his bank account.

Webb's office was filled with what I now realized might be additional forgeries. His reaction to learning about the storage unit was explosive.

"They destroyed the original to create a fake?" he shouted, his face turning red. "They took a priceless Thomas Cole painting and scraped it away to make a canvas for a forgery?"

"Well, it was damaged," I replied, "but yes, that's exactly what they did," I confirmed, showing him the photographs from the storage unit. "It looked pretty bad to me. That's fire damage, isn't it?"

He shook his head, obviously stunned. "But why? I don't understand."

Webb sank into his chair. He looked absolutely dumbfounded, physically sick. "How many other pieces?" he asked quietly.

"We're not sure," I said. "We're still analyzing the records, but... dozens."

"And the other pieces I bought from Lisa's gallery?"

"Again, I don't know," I replied. "We'll need to have them examined by an expert. If they match the pattern..." I trailed off. There was no need for me to say more.

Webb's devastation was complete. His carefully assembled collection of American art was potentially worthless.

With no little sorrow, I left Webb to deal with his financial and emotional losses and headed back to the department, thinking hard. I knew we needed expert help and, as a restorer herself, I figured Dr. Whitman was the obvious choice. That being so, I called her from the car and asked if she could come in to consult on the case. She said she'd be happy to do so and would be in my office no later than five o'clock. She arrived five minutes early.

To say I was surprised by her reaction when I briefed her would be something of an understatement: it was immediate and emotional.

"They destroyed 'The Painted Lady'?" she all but screamed, as she looked at the photographs with tears rolling down her face. "A Thomas Cole masterpiece? It's insane."

"I'm afraid so," I said. "But it was fire damaged." I showed her the photos. She didn't seem to care.

"That painting was irreplaceable," She wasn't quite sobbing, but it was close. "It was... it's like... It's like the burning of the Library of Alexandria."

Dr. Whitman's anguish was genuine and almost too painful to witness. Her obvious passion made what happened to the paintings seem that much more tragic.

"Dr. Whitman, I need your expertise. I need you to take a look at Marcus Webb's collection. We need to confirm the rest of the paintings he bought from Lisa are genuine... or not."

She looked up at me through watery eyes. "What can I do to help?"

"Well, first, I'm trying to figure out who had the knowledge and materials to commit these crimes—"

"Captain, I preserve artwork," she snapped angrily. "I don't destroy it, and I certainly don't kill people. But..." she paused, wiping her eyes. "But I understand why someone might want to stop this. What they were doing was monstrous." She was distraught.

Samson went to Dr. Whitman and put his head on her knee, offering comfort in his own gentle way.

Then she said almost absently, "Of course," she sniffled, stroking his head. "I'll look at Mr. Webb's paintings. I told you, I'll do what I can to help."

I let Dr. Whitman compose herself and thanked her for her help. Her expertise would be crucial for documenting the cultural significance of the destroyed pieces for the prosecution. After she left, I decided to inform Professor Patterson about what we'd discovered. As Sophia's thesis advisor, I figured, he too, deserved to know the full scope of what his student had been investigating.

BRUSHSTROKES AND BLOODLINES

THE FOLLOWING MORNING, AT JUST AFTER NINE, ALONG WITH Corbin and Samson, I visited Professor Patterson in his office at UTC. His reaction to learning about the storage unit was... different to that of Dr. Whitman, but no less intense. When I showed him the photographs and documentation, his academic composure collapsed completely.

"Sophia was right," he said, shaking his head in disbelief. "She suspected something like this, but the scale... I never imagined it was this extensive."

His hands trembled as he flipped through the photos I'd taken. The destruction of what he considered historical artwork clearly affected him.

"Professor, I need to know everything Sophia told you," I said. "And if you don't mind, I'm going to record the interview."

He nodded absentmindedly as he continued scrolling through the photographs. "She'd identified several pieces with what she called inconsistencies," he began. "She said the technical analysis didn't match what she'd expect, but the canvas dating was accurate. She'd seen 'The Painted Lady' in

Lisa Reynolds' gallery several weeks before Marcus Webb purchased it, and she told me she thought there was something about it that wasn't quite right. Apparently, she'd asked Lisa if she could examine it. Of course, Lisa refused, which only made Sophia that much more suspicious. Just before she disappeared, she told me she was going to ask Webb if she could have it examined." He looked up at me, cocked his head to one side and said, "That's it. That's all I know."

"That's quite a lot, Professor," I said. "And after she disappeared, as you put it, it should have raised at least one red flag."

Patterson rubbed his temples. "In retrospect, yes, I suppose it should have. But I must admit I thought Sophia was being overly critical."

"What about Jake Williams?" I asked.

"You never suspected he might be involved in fraud?" Corbin asked.

"Never," he replied. "He was quite a talented restorer. Not for a moment did I think he was using them to create forgeries."

"What d'you think Sophia was planning to do with her research?" I asked.

"I'm not sure," he replied. "She was a very serious young woman, quiet, dedicated. Her interaction with me was more one of... I think she was using me as a sounding board, looking for confirmation, so to speak. Perhaps she was building a case. She was certainly systematic about documentation of the irregularities she'd found. Perhaps she planned to present her findings to the academic community. Perhaps she was planning to publish. After all, it is what we academics do. Isn't it?"

Patterson walked to his window, and stood for a moment, staring out at the campus. "She was certainly going to do something with it," he muttered. "I recall she once told me, quite early in her investigations, that it would make her career, establish her as a serious researcher. Instead, it looks like it got her killed."

"Did she ever mention being threatened?" Corbin asked.

He nodded. "She was excited about her research but also concerned about the implications of what she was doing. She knew that a lot of people were going to be upset when the truth came out. As for direct threats, she twice mentioned getting an anonymous phone call telling her to stop what she was doing. Unfortunately, the only effect they had on her was to make her more determined. She said they validated her research."

"D'you know if she recorded these calls?" I asked.

"I don't think so," he replied. "But she did say that the person calling used a voice modulator or something. Made them sound robotic, she said."

I thought for a moment, then said, "Professor, I need a list of everyone in the area with the artistic skill and knowledge to create these historical forgeries."

"That's... that's a short list," he muttered. "It would require graduate-level training at a minimum, probably advanced degrees. You'd need to understand historical painting techniques, pigment chemistry, canvas preparation, and... and skill, an inordinate amount of skill."

"Names, Professor," I said.

He walked to his desk and took out a legal pad. "Dr. Angela Foster at Chattanooga State, obviously," he began. "Dr. Sarah Coleman; she does forensic art analysis. Vincent Harper, but he seems to be missing. And there are maybe six or seven others I can think of with the technical knowledge and skill set." He continued to write.

I waited until he stopped writing, then said, "What about students? Graduate students with exceptional talent?"

Patterson turned the corners of his mouth down as he

thought, his pen hovering over the paper. "A few, perhaps, but creating forgeries of this quality... it takes years of experience, not just talent."

He tore the sheet from the notepad and handed it to me. I glanced at it, folded it and put it into my jacket pocket, then I looked at my watch. It was already past ten-thirty.

I stood. So did Samson; then Corbin. I handed Patterson my card and asked him to call me if he thought of anything else, and then we took our leave of him.

"So, what do you think?' Corbin asked as we walked to my unmarked SUV.

"I think our girl got herself in way over her head," I said. "Either she bolted and is hiding out somewhere, or she's dead."

Corbin sighed and said, "So, what next?"

"Father Michael Blake, I think."

———————

WE FOUND Father Blake in his office behind the sanctuary, working on a grant application for his youth program.

"Good morning, Captain," he said after I knocked on the doorframe and entered. "What can I do for you today?"

I introduced Corbin—Samson he already knew—and then filled him in on what we'd found in the storage unit and its implications.

His first reaction was stunned silence. His second concern was for his young artists who'd worked at the gallery.

"These kids had no idea what they were witnessing," he said, setting aside his paperwork. "They were just grateful for jobs that let them enter the world of professional art."

"Did any of them ever mention seeing damaged paintings?" I asked.

He frowned, nodding slowly. "I do recall one boy mentioning he'd seen several paintings that looked like they'd been in fires or floods. He told me he was told they were in for restoration."

"I need the boy's name, please, Father," I said.

Father Blake stood and walked to his display case filled with pottery, paintings, and small sculptures created by his students and stared at them, obviously thinking.

"I'm not sure I can do that, Captain," he said. "I can't have my youngsters—"

"You can't refuse, Father," Corbin said, gently interrupting him. "To do so would be obstruction. Not good for you or the church."

Blake turned and looked at him, seemed to come to a decision, then nodded. "Tommy Flowers," he said. "He worked at Lisa's gallery for six months. He kept talking about how amazing it was to watch damaged paintings get 'restored' to look brand new."

"So he must have seen the finished work, then?" I asked.

"He did. He said the restoration brought the paintings to life, making them look like new. I didn't think anything of it at the time. I've seen restored paintings myself. They do indeed look bright and... well, like new."

The irony was heartbreaking. These young people had believed they were helping preserve cultural heritage when they were actually witnessing its destruction. The thought was... mind-boggling.

"Father, I need to talk to Tommy and any other kids who worked at the Reynolds gallery."

"Of course. But please be gentle with them. When they learn what they were really part of..."

"I understand. We'll handle it carefully."

"Captain, there is something else. One of my kids, Mary Yarber, she's studying art at Chattanooga State. She mentioned something odd a few months ago about someone offering cash for help with 'historical recreation projects.'"

"What kind of help?" I asked, frowning.

"Basic painting tasks, mixing pigments, preparing canvases. She turned it down because it interfered with her class schedule, but she said the money was really good."

"Did she say who made the offer?" Corbin asked.

"No, but she got the referral from someone at school. Another student, I think."

I made a note to follow up with Mary Yarber, and we left.

BACK AT THE DEPARTMENT, Jack had been diving deeper into Chattanooga's art world.

"Vincent Harper," he said, looking up at me. "He seems to be the man if you're wanting a painting authenticated. Apparently, he's board certified, and without his certificate, a forgery would have been worthless. If he's satisfied a painting is authentic, he will provide full scientific analysis reports, including canvas dating, paint composition, and provenance documentation. He's essentially been certifying that the forgeries were authentic historical pieces."

Jack pulled up more files on his computer. "But here's what's interesting: I've been going through Harper's phone records. He was obviously in on the deal because his last half-dozen emails to Lisa show he was becoming increasingly concerned about the scope of the operation. For instance, his last one, time-stamped three weeks ago, says— and he read the email out load, 'This is too much, Lisa. It's getting out of hand. People are asking questions. We need to slow it down. If we get hit with an independent audit, this thing will implode.'" He looked up at me. "Harper obviously wanted to scale back, to limit the number of pieces they were processing."

"And now he's missing," I said. "Any idea where he might be?"

Jack shook his head. "His digital footprint ended the day after he sent that email. None of his credit cards have been used since then either, and there are no calls in his phone records. He's either in the wind or he's dead," Jack replied. "I think he may have done a runner, though. He withdrew twenty thousand dollars in cash three days before he was last seen."

"So, he's on the run," I muttered.

"That's what I'm thinking," Jack said. "He knew things were getting out of hand and got out before it got worse."

Jack's continuing analysis revealed something else troubling. "And then there's this," he said. "The gallery bank records show large payments to six people—wire transfers. They're not as regular as those paid to Jake, but scattered across the last two years. I'm thinking they might be finder's fees, like they were finding and purchasing damaged pieces for Lisa and Jake."

"You think they're scouts?" I asked, frowning.

"I don't know," he replied. "It's just a theory, but I think it makes sense. I mean, if they could identify damaged pieces in private collections, estate sales, and the like…" He trailed off, but I could see the logic in his theory.

I nodded slowly, thinking, then said, "Wire transfers… So they pay for the artwork and keep what's left over?"

"No, I don't think it worked like that. I'm thinking the payments were flat finder's fees. Ten to twenty percent of the purchase price of the damaged pieces. Some of these scouts made thousands of dollars over the past two years; some of them not so much. As to the paintings themselves, the bank records show the gallery paid out sums up to thirty thousand over the same period; some to individuals, some to auction houses, five to museums. Sixty-one in all."

I bit my tongue, wondering what the hell they were thinking. They hadn't been shy about record keeping. *Payments made through banks?* I thought. It was almost arrogant, the way they'd gone about it. Even a cursory glance at their records would have revealed what they were doing. *But would they?* I thought. *Maybe the transparency was part of the deception.*

It was then that Tracy arrived. She took the seat to Jack's left, leaned forward and stared at his screens. "Yeah, I see it," she said. "I found similar patterns. The money trail is far from complex. It makes you wonder if they thought what they were doing was legit."

"Any leads on who might have been doing the actual painting yet?" I asked.

Jack shook his head. "There are checks written to local art supply stores; expensive stuff, not the stuff students or your local artists and such would buy."

"I visited three art supply stores this afternoon," Tracy said. "I showed them photos of Lisa, Jake, and Vincent Harper. Employees at two of the stores recognized Jake, but he was always buying restoration supplies. I asked if anyone had been purchasing anything out of the ordinary. But no one had."

THE HUNT FOR THE FORGER

CARMEN RODRIGUEZ ARRIVED IN MY OFFICE AT JUST AFTER four o'clock the following afternoon with a stack of files that painted an even grimmer picture.

"You don't mind, I take it," she said as the officer who brought her up closed the door behind him.

"Of course not," I replied. "Please sit down."

I cleared space on my desk as she settled into the chair across from me. Samson rose from his bed, sauntered over to her, and took up his usual position beside her chair.

Carmen looked tired, as if she'd been working nonstop since our last conversation.

"Coffee?" I offered, but she shook her head.

"I've had enough caffeine today to power a small city," she said, opening her briefcase. "Kate, what we found at that storage unit? It's... It's... I don't know what it is. Just the fact that they were destroying original pieces is bad enough, but doing it to create forgeries... It blows my mind. The financial implications are incalculable."

She took a sheaf of papers from her briefcase and spread

them across my desk. At a glance, I could see they were insurance claims.

"These are claims lodged against my company by individual collectors for forgeries purchased as the genuine article," she said, leaning back in her chair. "They won't mean much to you, but they show the scope of what those two were doing. I've been working with other insurance investigators across the Southeast. Atlanta, Birmingham, Nashville. High-value pieces bought through the Reynolds Gallery; all of them fakes."

I didn't know what to say, but I wasn't surprised.

"Regional American pieces," she continued. "Even an English piece. Most of them are 19th-century paintings with strong local historical connections. Someone was targeting artwork that would appeal to Southern collectors."

Again, I simply shook my head.

"Federal charges are inevitable," she said. "Interstate criminal commerce, high-end forgeries, conspiracy, you name it. The FBI's Art Crime Team is already expressing interest."

I almost smiled at that; almost, but not quite. Instead, I said, "It's going to be hard to bring any of those charges against Lisa and Jake; they're both dead, and Vincent Harper is either dead or in the wind. All that's left, as far as we know, is the artist and the killer. And we don't yet know who they are."

No, I wasn't being flippant, but her claim forms held little interest for me. I already knew the length and breadth of the crimes, but Carmen's revelation about federal involvement added a certain urgency to our investigation. Once the FBI took over, we'd be shut out and local leads would get lost in a larger investigation.

Carmen left some ten minutes later, more frustrated than when she arrived, and I felt for her. Frustration is a major part of what I do, what my team does. Day after day the frustration builds until, at last, something breaks. We just have to keep pushing forward until it does.

After she left, I remained seated at my desk, my arms folded, staring at the two whiteboards, both still annoyingly... white. There were photos on them, of course, held in place by magnets dressed up as pins. Lisa, Jake, Sophia, Harper, Webb... *Webb*, I thought. *I wonder!* And then I called Dr. Whitman.

Dr. Whitman had agreed to examine Marcus Webb's collection to determine which pieces might be forgeries. That was three days ago.

"Dr. Whitman," I said when she picked up. "This is Captain Gazzara. I was wondering. Is there any word on the authenticity of Marcus Webb's paintings?"

There wasn't, but she agreed to meet me at Webb's downtown office the following morning at eleven o'clock.

I ARRIVED on time to find Dr. Whitman already hard at work. Webb had not yet arrived.

Webb's suite of offices occupied the top floor of a renovated warehouse, with floor-to-ceiling windows overlooking the Tennessee River. His collection was displayed throughout the space - paintings, sculptures, and artifacts representing what he'd thought was a comprehensive representation of Southern art history.

Webb arrived two or three minutes after I did.

"I've been here since eight this morning," Whitman reported, setting down a powerful magnifying glass. "Your PA let me in." She paused for a moment, looking tired but focused. Finally, she looked at him and said, "I'm sorry to have to tell you, Mr. Webb, that of the twelve paintings you purchased from Lisa Reynold's gallery, seven are forgeries."

Webb sat heavily in his leather chair, his face ashen. "Seven out of twelve?"

"I'm afraid so," she replied. "The good news is that five are genuine pieces. They appear to have been legitimately acquired and are quite valuable."

"But the forgeries?"

"Worthless as investments, but from a technical standpoint they're actually quite good. Whoever painted them understood historical techniques remarkably well."

Dr. Whitman walked me through her analysis, pointing out the telltale signs that distinguished the forgeries from authentic pieces. "The brushwork is excellent, the color palette is accurate for the period, and even the aging of the pigment appears natural. But there are subtle differences in paint application that suggest modern training."

"Modern training? What d'you mean? Painting is painting, isn't it?"

At that, she smiled. "No, Captain. Contemporary art education emphasizes different techniques than those used by historical artists. The forger understood historical methods intellectually, but the muscle memory came from modern training."

"So what does that tell us?" I asked.

"We're looking for someone with formal art education who also studied historical techniques extensively," she replied. "Probably graduate-level work in art history or conservation."

"How many people in Chattanooga would fit that profile?"

"Not many," she replied. "Maybe a dozen people with the technical knowledge, but fewer still with the actual artistic skill to pull it off."

Dr. Whitman had brought with her a list she'd compiled of local artists with the necessary expertise. "Art professors at local universities, professional conservators, and a few independent artists with advanced training."

I studied the list. Most of the people we'd already encountered during the investigation were on it, including Patterson and Foster, but there were several names I didn't recognize.

"Dr. Whitman, what about graduate students?" I asked. "Someone currently enrolled in an advanced program?"

"Possible, but unlikely. This level of technical skill usually takes years to develop after formal education."

"But if someone was exceptionally talented?" I pressed her.

She pondered the question for a moment. "There are always exceptional students. Someone with natural ability and intensive study of historical techniques... it's possible, I suppose."

As Dr. Whitman packed up her equipment, I could see she was genuinely saddened about the destroyed artwork. Her passion for cultural preservation was obvious and admirable.

"Dr. Whitman, thank you for your help," I said. "Your expertise has been invaluable."

She shrugged. "You're welcome, Captain. I wish we'd met under better circumstances. This kind of cultural vandalism... well, it's very personal for people like me. These pieces represented centuries of artistic achievement, and they were destroyed for money. It's disgusting."

"Dr. Whitman," I said, "one more question, if you please. If you wanted to find the forger, where would you look?"

"Art supply stores first. The materials needed for this work are specialized and expensive. Second, art schools. Someone with this level of skill probably studied locally. Third, the gallery connection. The forger had to have known Lisa and probably Jake, too. And whoever it was certainly knew about the operation."

"If you were me, where would you start?" I asked.

Chapter 7

"I'd begin with the graduate programs in art history and conservation. Cross-reference with anyone who's worked with historical pigments and/or studied 19th-century techniques. Now, I hate to run, but I have an appointment at two, and I need some lunch. So, if you'll excuse me..."

I thanked her again; we said our goodbyes, and she hurried away looking a little like Professor McGonagall, minus the pointy hat, of course.

I left Webb staring soulfully at his paintings—they all looked damn good to me, but what do I know?—and drove back to the department thinking about Dr. Whitman's suggestions. It was then I realized we could well have been approaching this from the criminal angle when what we really needed to do was think like art educators. Who had the knowledge, the skill and the opportunity?

I WAS ON AMNICOLA, but hadn't quite made it to the police department when I received a text from Grace Parker, so I pulled over and read it. She was requesting another meeting, claiming she'd uncovered additional information through her blog research and that she was at the same coffee shop as before.

I looked at my watch. It was almost one o'clock, and I realized I was hungry. So I turned around and headed back along Amnicola.

Grace was seated at a table by the window. She looked exhausted.

What's up with her? I wondered as I stepped up to the counter. I ordered a large coffee—black—and a slab of German chocolate cake. *There goes my diet!* I thought as I ordered a slab of pound cake for Sammy. "No chocolate for you, boy," I said, ignoring the stares from the other customers. Yes, Samson was, as always, wearing his K-9 harness and badge, so he was allowed in the coffee shop.

"I've been getting emails," she said as I sat down, turning her laptop so I could see the screen. "People responding to my blog posts about authentication fraud. Stories from all over the Southeast about similar problems."

I put Sammy's pound cake on a paper towel and set it down on the floor beside me.

"Stories?" I said skeptically. To tell the truth, I was weary, tired, and all this art crap was making my head spin. Now I was faced with yet another bunch of it. "What stories?" I asked, resignedly.

I picked up my coffee and sipped. *Damn! It's scalding hot.*

"Collectors mostly," she said. "People who discovered they'd been sold forgeries, museums that sold 'damaged' pieces to so-called conservators, even art students who'd been offered cash for mysterious projects."

Students who were offered cash? She had my interest. "Projects?" I asked. "Did you talk to any of them?"

"We texted," she replied. "There were two emails that mention a woman who approached art students with offers to work on restoration projects."

"Restoration projects," I repeated. "What's wrong with that? Do we have any descriptions?" I asked.

She shrugged. "Well, no, there's nothing wrong with it. I'm just saying. They were to be on the lookout for damaged paintings. If they found any, they were to be paid in cash."

"And the description?" I pressed her.

"A young woman, maybe late twenties, brown hair, very knowledgeable about art history. She always paid in cash, never gave contact information other than a first name."

"And that name is?" I asked.

"Mickey, like the mouse."

"That it?" I asked.

"That's it," she said, nodding. "I hope it helps."

But would it? Grace had told me nothing I didn't already know other than a name. *Mickey?* I thought. *Nope! Nothing! Damn it!*

We spent the next ten minutes rehashing what we'd already gone over while I finished my coffee and cake. Sammy, as you might imagine, had devoured his pound cake in record time and was sitting quietly at my side.

So, I finished up, thanked Grace for her help, and then I resumed my journey back to the police department on Amnicola.

THE NEIGHBOR'S SECRET

THE BREAKTHROUGH CAME THE FOLLOWING MORNING WHEN I was reviewing Tony's recorded interview with Michelle Parry for the fourth time. Something about her responses had been nagging at me for days, but I couldn't put my finger on exactly what it was. It was mid-morning. I had my office door open, as I usually did, and the situation room was relatively quiet: just the usual sounds of phones ringing and keyboards clicking.

"Tracy," I called across the situation room, too lazy to pick up the phone and tap in her number. "Come listen to this. I need a fresh perspective."

She pulled up a chair next to my desk as I replayed the section where Michelle described Sophia's research methods. The recording quality was good. Tony's digital recorder had captured every nuance of Michelle's voice.

"She was incredibly organized," Michelle's voice came through the speaker. "Everything had to be documented, photographed, and cross-referenced. She kept saying that when you're challenging established authentications, you need bulletproof evidence."

Chapter 8

"What am I listening for?" Tracy asked, settling into her chair with a cup of coffee.

"The level of detail. Don't you think Michelle knew way too much about Sophia's specific research methods? A concerned neighbor might know Sophia was working on something important, but listen to how precisely she describes the documentation process."

I forwarded to another section. "She told me she'd been getting calls from someone she couldn't identify. She said they were related to her research. And she'd started locking her door, which wasn't like her."

Tracy frowned. "Sorry, I'm still not seeing the problem."

"A concerned neighbor might know Sophia was getting mysterious calls. But how would she know the calls were specifically related to Sophia's research? And how would she know Sophia's door-locking habits well enough to say it 'wasn't like her'?"

"You think Michelle knows more than she lets on?" Tracy asked, frowning.

"I think Michelle knew exactly what Sophia was researching," I said.

I pulled up Michelle Parry's academic file on my computer. Fine arts major. Specialization: historical painting techniques. Particular focus: 19th-century American artists.

"A graduate student with no apparent source of income," I said. "How's she paying for tuition, board and lodging, and supplies?"

"Wealthy parents?" Tracy said, grinning.

I ignored that. "Look at this," I said, pointing to the screen. "She's been studying the exact same techniques and historical periods as the forgeries."

"That could be coincidence," Tracy said, leaning back in her chair, then taking a sip of her coffee.

"Oh, come on, Tracy. We don't believe in coincidences."

"So you say," Tracy replied, "but they happen often enough."

I stared at her across my desk as she flipped a wisp of black hair from in front of her eyes. I made duck lips, tilted my head to the right, and watched her raise her eyebrows and smile at me.

"You really think it could be a coincidence?" I asked skeptically.

"Could be," she replied, taking another sip of her coffee.

"But combined with her detailed knowledge of Sophia's research and her convenient position as the helpful neighbor..." I trailed off, thinking.

"Tracy," I said finally. "Go run Michelle Parry through our financial database. Look for any payments from Lisa's gallery or connections to Jake Williams."

While Tracy went to work at her computer, I called Jack North. "Jack, I need you to cross-reference all the financial records from the forgery operation. Look for any payments to M. Parry, Michelle Parry, or any Parry at all."

"What are you thinking, Cap?" he asked.

"I'm thinking our helpful neighbor might be more involved in this than she'd like us to think. How long will it take?"

"Give me twenty minutes," he said and hung up.

I sat back in my chair, thinking about Michelle's interview. Her detailed knowledge of Sophia's research methods, her convenient position as the neighboring witness, her artistic background, but was she capable of creating sophisticated forgeries? The more I thought about it, the more convinced I became that we'd been looking at this case backwards.

"Kate," Tracy called from her computer terminal. "Got something. A Michelle Parry has been making regular cash deposits into an out-of-state bank for the past two years.

Small amounts, but consistent. Total of about one hundred and two thousand dollars."

"What's the source? And is it our Michelle Parry?"

She came to my office and leaned on the door frame, her hand above her head, grasping the woodwork. "Source unknown," she said. "Same nosey neighbor? I don't know. Always cash deposits, no check or transfer records. But the timing of the deposits kinda matches up with the timeline of the forgery operation."

Hmm, that's interesting. I thought. *A graduate student with no apparent source of income wouldn't normally have a hundred thousand dollars in the bank; that's if she's our graduate student.*

"What's the pattern?" I asked.

"Monthly deposits, usually between three and five thousand dollars. Never the same amount, never on the same day of the month, but consistently every month for the past twenty-four months. But, Kate, it doesn't make sense. If this is our forger, she'd be making a whole lot more than five thousand a month, wouldn't she?"

I blew out through my lips and shook my head. She was right, of course. It didn't make sense.

"Okay, Tracy. Keep digging. I need to know who your Michelle Parry really is."

She nodded and went back to her desk.

Jack called back fifteen minutes later, and I could hear excitement in his voice. "Kate, you're going to want to see this. I found payments from Lisa's gallery to 'M. Parry' for 'restoration work.' Eighteen payments over two years, totaling exactly one-hundred-forty thousand dollars."

And there it was, or so I thought. Michelle Parry, Sophia's helpful neighbor, was the forger we'd been searching for. Or was it? One-hundred-forty thousand still wasn't much for what she was doing. And if she was Tracy's Michelle Parry, she was keeping a little back to cover expenses, I presumed. *Geez*, I thought, *maybe she's doing it for the love of it.*

"Jack, can you tell me exactly when these payments were made?" I asked.

"The payments started about six months after Michelle enrolled in graduate school. The last payment was three weeks ago, right before Lisa Reynolds was murdered."

"What were the payment amounts?"

"Started small - five hundred, eight hundred dollars. By the end, they were paying her up to ten thousand. That was the amount of the last payment."

"So they started small," I said, thoughtfully. "They got their feet wet, so to speak, then slowly extended their range until they were reproducing masters."

I called an emergency briefing with the entire team. Within twenty minutes, everyone was assembled in the conference room - Tracy, Corbin, Tony, and Jack North. Hawk was out of town attending a funeral and wouldn't be back for a couple of days.

"We've been looking at this case from the wrong angle," I announced, pointing at the financial records spread across the table. "It seems Sophia's next-door neighbor, Michelle Parry is the forger we've been looking for."

Corbin looked skeptical. "That nice young woman who provided all that useful information about Sophia's research? You're kidding, right?"

"No, I'm not kidding. Think about it," I said, pulling up Michelle's academic records on my desktop and turning it for them to see. "She knew details about Sophia's research that no casual neighbor would know. She has advanced artistic training specifically in historical painting techniques. And she's been receiving regular payments from Lisa's gallery for 'restoration work.'"

"I still don't believe it," Tracy said. "The payments are

recorded as 'for restoration work.' The size of the payments reflects exactly that, restoration work. Hell, the girl had to make a living somehow, and she certainly didn't hide it, which is what a criminal would have done."

"Maybe she's smart," I replied. "Maybe she didn't hide the payments for just that reason."

Tony was reviewing his interview notes. "Geez, if what you're saying is true, I missed it completely. She played me."

"Don't beat yourself up," I said. "Her performance was pretty damn good. And I think she knew exactly what Sophia had discovered because she was part of the operation Sophia was investigating."

Tracy was still studying the financial records, still shaking her head. "Look, if what you say is true, if Michelle was the forger, she'd have known Sophia was getting too close to the truth, and she's smart enough to have cleaned up her act. After all, as far as I see, the only link you have is the money transfers."

"Exactly. And she'd know exactly what evidence Sophia had gathered," I said. "Remember those anonymous phone calls warning Sophia to stop her investigation? I'm betting Michelle made those calls."

"So, what you're saying is that Michelle tried to warn Sophia off, and when that didn't work..." Corbin trailed off.

"She told Lisa and Jake that Sophia was onto them, which led to Sophia's murder," I finished for him.

Jack, who was also analyzing the payment patterns on his laptop, looked up and said, "The last payment to Michelle was three weeks ago, just before Sophia went missing, and ten days before Lisa Reynolds was murdered."

"I think she's been lying to us from the beginning," I said, that deep-seated feeling in my gut pushing me onward. "The question is, what else does she know? And is she our killer?"

I assigned tasks to each team member. "Tony, I want you

to review every word of your interview with Michelle. Look for inconsistencies, details that don't match what we now know. Tracy, dig deeper into Michelle's finances. I want to know where every dollar came from and where it went. Are there more payments we don't know about? Jack, cross-reference Michelle's academic schedule with the timeline of the forgery operation. Corbin, you're with me."

"Where are we going?" he asked, rising quickly to his feet.

"To have another conversation with Michelle Parry. This time, she's going to tell us the truth. Come on, Sammy."

AN HOUR LATER, we were standing outside Michelle's apartment building. Looking up at the windows. "I'm certain she's the forger, Corbin," I said. "Michelle? Mickey? Why not? They lived next door to one another. She had easy access to Sophia's apartment. Maybe she could even hear her through the walls."

"How do you want to play this?" Corbin asked as we approached the main entrance.

"Careful but direct," I said. "We don't want to spook her. She may be our best source of information about what really happened to Sophia."

I knocked on Michelle's door. It opened a moment later to reveal the young woman. She was as Tony described her: brown hair, maybe late twenties, perky.

"Michelle Parry?" I asked.

"Yes..." She drew the word out, frowning.

"I'm Captain Gazzara, Chattanooga police. This is Sergeant Russell. Don't mind the dog. He won't hurt you. We'd like to ask you some follow-up questions to your previous interview."

"Captain Gazzara," she said, "of course, please come on

in." She glanced nervously at Samson as she stepped aside to let us by. "I told the officer all I know. I don't see how I can help…" she trailed off. Then said, "Please… sit down."

Her apartment was small. Shelves lined one wall of the main room, filled with art supplies and historical painting references. Canvases in various stages of completion were stacked against the walls. Even unfinished, it was easy to see the quality of her work.

She seated herself at the end of the sofa, her hands clasped together in her lap. Corbin took the chair opposite her, and I sat at the table, watching her carefully.

"For the record, Michelle," I began as I set my phone to record, "I'm going to record our conversation, if that's all right with you."

She nodded.

"Out loud, please," I said.

"Yes, of course. Please do," she said.

"We need to talk to you about your relationships with Lisa Reynolds and Jake Williams," I said.

At that, she frowned and narrowed her eyes almost to slits. "I don't know what you mean," she said.

I leaned forward. "Come on, Michelle," I said gently. "Give it up. We know about the payments. One-hundred-forty thousand dollars over two years for restoration work. You're the forger, aren't you?"

She sat stock-still for a moment, only her eyes moving, darting back and forth between Corbin and me. I could tell I'd hit a nerve. And I figured she must be desperately trying to decide if further deception was possible.

"I never meant for anyone to get hurt," she said, lowering her head to stare at the floor. "Will I go to jail?"

I ignored the question. "Tell me about the forgeries, Michelle."

She took a deep breath, and I watched her shoulders slump.

"I was desperate for money," she said without looking up. "Graduate school, rent, art supplies... I was drowning in debt. My parents couldn't help, and I was working three part-time jobs just to make minimum payments on my student loans." She heaved a huge, shuddering breath, looked up at me with tears in her eyes, and reached down to stroke Samson's head.

"How did Lisa Reynolds find you?" I asked.

"Through Professor Foster," she replied. "I don't think she knew what Lisa was doing. She just mentioned that one of her best students was struggling financially and had a feel for restoration work. That was it, really. She offered me some restoration work, and one thing... led... to... another."

"Go one," I said.

"At first, it seemed completely legitimate. Lisa said she had several damaged historical pieces that needed repair and asked if it was something I could do. Well, of course it was, though many of the pieces were beyond redemption, and I jumped at the chance. I worked several pieces for her, then she asked me to work a piece that she claimed had been in a fire. It was a small piece—eight by ten—and all the pigment had been removed down to the canvas. It still had its frame and brass plate, and she had a photo of the original. She called it 'historical recreation; I remember it well. It was by Eugene Walsh, 1877, Spanish Lady. I also remember thinking that what I was doing was forgery. I even said so to Lisa, but she brushed it off, saying again that it was historical recreation."

"What did she pay you?"

"More than I'd ever seen. Seven-hundred-fifty dollars for that first piece, which took me about a week to complete. That was double what I made at my three part-time jobs."

"When did you realize what was really happening?" Corbin asked kindly.

Michelle wiped tears from her eyes. "When I started seeing my work being sold as authentic pieces rather than reproductions. Lisa told me they were just study reproductions for academic research, but then I saw them in authentication reports, being sold for hundreds of thousands of dollars."

"How did that make you feel?" he asked.

"Terrified. I knew what I was doing was wrong, but Lisa wouldn't have it. She said there were many levels of restoration and that what I was doing was just one of them."

"Why didn't you stop when you realized what was happening?" I asked.

"I tried," she said. "I told Lisa I wanted out, that I couldn't be part of fraud. But by then, I was trapped."

"Trapped?" I asked, though I knew the answer. Once you're in, there's no way out.

"Lisa finally admitted what we were doing was wrong, and Jake said I was as guilty as they were, that I'd go to prison as an accomplice if anyone found out. They had documentation of all my work, all the payments they'd made to me. They said they'd destroy my academic career, and I'd be prosecuted for fraud."

"But they kept paying you," I said.

"Yes," she replied. "The amounts got larger as my forgeries got more sophisticated. By the end, I was making more money in a month than most people make in a year."

"And then Sophia happened," I said.

At that, her composure cracked completely, and she began to sob. "When Sophia started asking questions about authentication irregularities, I got scared; I mean I was terrified. She was smart, methodical, and she was focusing on the pieces I'd worked on."

"So you tried to warn her off," Corbin said.

"I made a couple of anonymous calls. I disguised my voice and told her to stop. I thought if she backed off, everyone would be safe."

"But she didn't back off, did she?" Corbin asked.

"No. She was determined to expose the fraud. She said she had a moral obligation to protect historical artwork."

I leaned forward in my chair. "Michelle, I need you to tell me exactly what happened to Sophia."

"She confronted Lisa and Jake at the gallery. She had photographs, documentation, proof of the forgery operation. She knew about the destroyed paintings, the fake authentication certificates, everything."

"Were you there?" I asked.

"No, but Jake called me afterward. He was terrified. He said Sophia had threatened to go public with everything, and to contact law enforcement."

"What was Lisa's reaction?" I asked.

"Jake said Lisa lost it completely, that she started screaming about her business, her reputation, her financial investments. But Sophia wouldn't back down."

"Did they kill Sophia?" Corbin asked gently. Samson wriggled at her feet.

Michelle took several deep breaths before continuing. "Jake said Lisa grabbed a gun from the desk drawer and shot her in the head. He said he tried to help her, but she was already dead."

She looked at me. Tears were streaming down her cheeks. Her chest was heaving. She was in full panic mode. "I don't know if that's what really happened, Captain. I wasn't there."

I nodded slowly. I was certain she wasn't, but I wasn't going to let her off the hook. "Do you know what they did with Sophia's body, Michelle?"

"Jake told me they took her to the county landfill. He said

he knew someone who worked there, someone who could make sure the body was buried deep enough that it would never be found. I think he had to pay the man a lot of money."

Michelle's confession confirmed what I'd suspected about her role as the forger. More importantly, it gave us the location of Sophia's remains, which would provide closure for her family and physical evidence to document what had really happened.

"Michelle, I need you to come with us for formal questioning and protective custody."

"Protective custody? Why?"

"Because you've confessed to a crime and because someone's been killing people—Lisa and Jake and perhaps others —connected to the forgery operation, and you could be next." By 'others,' I had Vincent Harper in mind.

The booking process took longer than usual. Michelle Parry sat quietly in the holding area while the paperwork was processed, her earlier tears dried but her face still showing the strain of her confession. I'd arranged for her to be placed in protective custody rather than general population. If someone *was* systematically eliminating everyone connected to the forgery operation, I figured Michelle had to be on the list.

"She'll be safe here," Sergeant Martinez assured me as we completed the forms and I signed off on them. "We've got her in the secure wing with round-the-clock supervision."

I thought about that for a minute, then took him to one side and whispered, "I suggest you put her on suicide watch. She's an artist and way overemotional."

He glanced round at her, then looked again at me and said, "You got it, Captain."

"Good. And Martinez? No visitors without my approval. No phone calls except to her attorney. Someone out there knows she's the forger, and I don't want them getting to her."

"Understood, Captain."

I left Michelle in the capable hands of the booking officers and headed home, my mind churning with everything she'd revealed. Sophia Blake had died trying to expose cultural vandalism. And somewhere out there, someone was killing off the participants.

The drive home through Chattanooga's quiet streets gave me time to think. Michelle's confession had answered a lot of questions about the forgery operation, but it had also raised some new ones. Who was eliminating the network members? How did they know about the operation? And why were they taking justice into their own hands?

By the time I pulled into my driveway, exhaustion was settling in. It had been a long day. We'd solved the forgery part of the case, and we'd solved Sophia's disappearance, but we hadn't found Harper and we hadn't found our killer; the case was far from over.

I pulled up outside my garage door and parked my SUV there for the night. Samson jumped across the console, over my lap and down onto the gravel driveway and ran to the grass verge and relieved himself, much to my amusement, then ran to join me at the front door. I opened it and he ran in, straight to the kitchen where he stood over his bowl giving me a baleful look.

"You're going to have to give me a minute, Sammy. I need to… Oh, what the hell?" I picked up his bowl, went to the cupboard and poured in six cups of kibble. He is, after all, a very big dog, and he hadn't eaten since morning.

That done, I went upstairs, stripped off my clothes, took a shower and dressed in clean sweats. Then I went back downstairs, noted the empty bowl, let Sammy out back and then went to the fridge. Where, like old Mother Hubbard, I found the cupboard bare, well, almost. There was half a pepperoni pizza on the bottom shelf, so I took it out, shoved it in the toaster oven and opened a bottle of red.

I let Sammy back in, poured myself a glass of wine, grabbed three slices of scalding hot pizza, then settled down on the couch in the living room where Sammy immediately joined me, his head on my lap.

And for the next hour, that's where I stayed. I ate my pizza, all three slices, drank the wine, and stared out of the window.

But, me being me, and things being what they were, it was inevitable that my mind wandered back to the case.

"What do you think, Sammy?" I asked. "We know Michelle was the forger. We know Lisa and Jake killed Sophia and disposed of her body at the county landfill. But who killed Jake and Lisa?"

Samson's eyes—his head still on my lap—constantly switched back and forth as he seemed to consider the question. And not for the first time since I had him, I told him I wished he could talk.

"It had to be someone who knew about the forgeries," I said. "They knew enough to target Lisa first, then Jake. They had access to both victims and the means to kill them. But who?"

I reviewed the timeline in my mind. Lisa Reynolds was found dead at her gallery, the scene staged to make it look like she committed suicide by gunshot. Jake Williams was found dead at his workshop, the victim of a violent stabbing with one of his own tools.

"The killer knew details about the operation, Sammy. They targeted Lisa and Jake specifically, and that suggests inside knowledge."

I stared blankly out the window. Chattanooga was

settling into evening quiet, but my mind was still racing through the possibilities.

"We've interviewed everyone connected to the case," I said, scratching his head. "Gallery owners, collectors, professors, museum experts. Someone we talked to knows more than they're letting on."

As I sat there thinking about our interviews, my mind drifted back to the beginning of the investigation. That first day at Lisa's gallery, reexamining the crime scene in my mind, trying to understand what had happened. Mike had secured and processed the scene. Dr. Whitman arrived to inspect the artwork, then Webb... *Hmm, Webb...* Then Doc arrived and... And then it hit me, something Dr. Whitman had said, "I just can't understand why she would shoot herself. She seemed to have everything going for her..."

I sat up straighter. "Wait a minute, Sammy. Dr. Whitman said Lisa shot herself. But how did she know?"

We hadn't determined the actual cause of death at that time. And yes, at that point we still thought she'd killed herself, but she, Whitman, said that even before Doc arrived and, to my certain knowledge, she never saw the body. And we sure as hell hadn't released any information to the media, nor to the public, nor to anyone outside the crime scene.

"How did she know Lisa died from a gunshot wound, Sammy?" I asked.

He lifted his head and cocked it to one side.

"As far as I know, nobody told her. I didn't tell her. The only people who knew were the police officers at the scene, the medical examiner, and... The killer."

I reached for my phone and dialed Corbin's number.

"Kate? What's up?"

"I know who it is," I said. "I know who killed Lisa and Jake."

THE FINAL CANVAS

"Who?" Corbin asked. I could hear him coughing, as if he'd just swallowed something that didn't agree with him.

"Dr. Patricia Whitman. Remember her?" I said. "We totally missed her. You remember she was there at Lisa's gallery the first day. She said... geez, something to the effect of—and I'm paraphrasing here—'I can't understand why she would shoot herself.' How would she know that Lisa died from a gunshot wound, Corbin?"

He was silent for a moment, then said, "You're right, Kate. Only the killer could know that. What do you want to do?"

I looked at my watch. It was almost eight o'clock. "She'll be home now," I said. "Get her address, text it to me, and meet me there."

"Hold on," he said. "Give me two minutes." I heard his keyboard clicking. "Got it. Lookout Mountain Road. Big house; looks like it's been in her family for years based on the property records. Texting it now. Twenty minutes?"

"Make it thirty," I said. "I have to get dressed."

"I'll be waiting," he replied. "Should we call for backup?"

I thought about it. Dr. Whitman had killed two people,

but she wasn't a violent criminal in the traditional sense. She'd been methodical, purposeful. If we approached this right, maybe we could avoid a confrontation.

"Not yet," I said. "Let's see what we're dealing with first. She's not going to run. At least I don't think she will. She's been hiding in plain sight all this time. I have a feeling she wants to be caught."

"Okay, but we know she's handy with a gun, so I'm bringing my vest just in case."

"Good idea. See you there."

I hung up and looked at Samson, who'd been watching me, cocking his head from one side to the other each time I spoke.

"Good boy, Sammy," I said, ruffling the long hair on the back of his neck. "Let's go finish this."

———————

THE DRIVE UP Lookout Mountain Road took me along winding roads lined with expensive homes, each one set back among stands of mature trees that provided privacy from the street. Dr. Whitman's house was a large Victorian-era mansion, old Chattanooga money and cultural refinement.

Corbin was waiting in his unmarked cruiser when I arrived. I pulled up behind him. He got out of the car, and I smiled to see he was already wearing his vest. I opened my door, unclipped Samson and, as usual, he scrambled over the console and down onto the ground and stood there looking up at me, his mouth open, tongue lolling out.

"Any signs of activity?" I asked.

"Lights are on in most of the downstairs rooms," he replied. "And there's a car in the driveway, so I guess she's home."

"Okay," I said. "Let's go see what she has to say for herself."

We walked up the brick pathway to the front door, past carefully maintained lawns and flower beds. The house itself was immaculate, newly painted white with black shutters— the real deal, not plastic.

I rang the doorbell and heard footsteps approaching from inside.

"Captain Gazzara," Dr. Whitman said when she opened the door. She didn't seem surprised to see us. "How nice. I've been expecting you. I was wondering when you'd figure it out. It was what I said in Lisa's gallery, wasn't it? I knew you'd latch onto it sooner or later. Later would have been better, but there it is."

She was dressed casually in slacks and a sweater, looking more like someone's favorite aunt than a double murderer. But her eyes held the same intense focus I'd noticed throughout our investigation.

I was stunned by her admission. "Dr. Whitman, we need to talk," I said, for want of something to say.

"Of course. Please come in."

She led us through a foyer lined with original artwork and into a large study that looked like something from a museum. Floor-to-ceiling bookshelves filled with art history texts, conservation manuals, and auction catalogs. Several easels held paintings in various stages of restoration, and the room smelled faintly of the same chemicals in Jake Williams' studio.

"Would you like some tea? Coffee?" she asked, as if we were social visitors.

"No, thank you, Dr. Whitman. You know why we're here," I said, taking out my phone and setting it to record.

Dr. Whitman smiled sadly. "Yes, indeed I do. I've been a little careless in my old age, I suppose."

Corbin had positioned himself near the door while I took a seat across from her. Samson settled beside my chair, his attention focused on Dr. Whitman.

"Patricia Whitman," I began, "I'm here to arrest you on suspicion of the murders of Lisa Reynolds and Jake Williams. You have the right to remain silent..." blah, blah, blah "...do you understand these rights?" I finished.

She nodded and said, "I do."

"With these rights in mind," I continued, "are you willing to speak with me?"

"Yes," she said, quietly, her head down.

"Why don't you tell us what happened," I said.

"Where would you like me to start? With Sophia's research, or with the night I watched them murder her?"

"You... you... what?" I asked, stunned.

"I saw Lisa shoot her in the head."

Frickin' hell! I thought, then took a deep breath and said, "Let's start with Sophia."

Dr. Whitman leaned back in her chair, her eyes focusing on a partially restored landscape painting on the nearby easel. "Sophia contacted me about six months ago. She was researching inconsistencies in local gallery sales and needed technical expertise to confirm her suspicions." She paused, looked pensively at me, then continued. "Over the next several months, she brought several pieces to me. How she got hold of them, I have no idea. She didn't tell me, and I didn't ask. Discretion was the basis of our relationship. Anyway, I provided a scientific analysis of the pieces she'd identified as questionable. Canvas dating, paint composition, authentication certificate verification and together, we documented fraud involving multiple paintings and three collectors."

"When did you realize the scope of the operation?" I asked.

"Gradually. At first, it seemed like typical authentication disputes: dealers cutting corners, buyers not doing proper due diligence. But as Sophia's research progressed, we uncovered something much worse."

Dr. Whitman stood and walked to a bookshelf, pulling out a thick folder. "By my count, twenty-seven historically significant paintings were destroyed over the last two years. I'm sure there were more, but these are the ones I was able to track down. Twenty-seven supposedly damaged pieces. Many of them purchased at rock-bottom prices. Damaged? Maybe. A little. Restorable? Some. Not all of them, I'm sure, but all were deliberately scraped down to the canvas to provide properly aged canvases for the forgeries."

She opened the folder, revealing photographs and documentation that rivaled anything our investigation had produced.

"This is 'The Painted Lady,'" she said, showing me a photograph of the Thomas Cole masterpiece before its destruction. "Painted in 1847, along with its two sister paintings, it documented Chattanooga's pre-Civil War cultural heritage. It survived the Civil War, Reconstruction, two World Wars, and the Great Depression. One hundred and seventy years of American history, only to be destroyed by criminals for profit."

Her voice grew harder as she continued. "Look at them. George Inness landscapes that influenced generations of American artists. Martin Johnson Heade paintings that captured unique moments in Southern history. All scraped away like old wallpaper."

"So you decided to take justice into your own hands."

"I decided that crimes against cultural heritage deserved appropriate consequences. The legal system treats art fraud as a property crime, but it's really cultural vandalism that affects all of humanity."

"Tell us about the night Sophia was killed," Corbin said.

Dr. Whitman returned to her chair, the folder still in her hands. "Sophia called me that evening. She said she had definitive proof of the forgery operation and needed my expertise to document it properly before contacting authorities. I was to meet her at Lisa's gallery. She was going to confront her."

Again she paused, as if she was collecting her thoughts.

"I arrived early and saw lights in the back," she continued. "When I looked through the rear window, I saw Sophia confronting Lisa Reynolds and Jake Williams. She was shouting at them."

"What did you do?" Corbin asked. "Did you go in?"

"I'm a bit of a coward, I'm afraid. So, no, I didn't go in. I listened at the window. Sophia was magnificent, brave, articulate, uncompromising. She told them that their operation was criminal and that they were destroying centuries of cultural heritage."

Dr. Whitman's composure cracked slightly as she relived the memory. "Lisa Reynolds became enraged. She started screaming about her business, her reputation, and her financial investments. But Sophia was adamant. She stated she was going to take her evidence to the police."

"So how was she killed?" I already knew from what Michelle had told us, but I wanted to verify her version by comparing it to Whitman's.

"Lisa was babbling with rage. She screamed something about…" she heaved a deep breath and continued, "something about not letting Sophia ruin her. She was behind her desk. She grabbed a pistol from the desk drawer—it was already open—and she came around the desk and shot Sophia in the head. Then she dropped the pistol and covered her mouth with both hands. I think she was stunned by what she'd done. Sophia collapsed instantly. Jake tried to help her, but she was already dead."

Her description of the murder was chilling.

"Why didn't you call the police?" I asked, unable to grasp the logic of her thinking.

"In retrospect, that's exactly what I should have done," she replied, "but I was both terrified and horrified. But more than that—and I know how this is going to sound—I was furious about the scope of the cultural destruction she'd discovered. I've been around this business long enough to know how it works, and that they'd only get a slap on the wrist and the destruction would continue if I didn't do something about it." She shrugged. "So that's what I decided I had to do. Like a real-life 'Punisher.'"

I couldn't believe what I was hearing. "So you planned revenge."

"Not revenge, justice," she replied. "At first, I intended to do it the right way. I tried to find legal channels that would adequately punish them, but the penalties were ludicrously pathetic."

She looked directly at me as she continued, "A few years in prison for destroying priceless historical artifacts? Fines for vandalism? It wasn't enough."

"What about the forgeries?" I asked. "That alone would have gotten them ten years."

"But they didn't forge them, did they?" she said. "Someone else did that. All they did was destroy the originals and then sell the forgeries. Without the forger, it would have been almost impossible to prove otherwise. And besides, a good attorney might even make the case that what they were doing wasn't forgery at all, just a complete restoration of the original. Oh yes. Don't look at me like that, young man. They were that good. What a waste of talent."

"Tell me about Lisa's murder," I said.

"I confronted her at the gallery two weeks after Sophia's death. I told her I knew what they were doing and that I'd seen her kill Sophia. I demanded that she stop the operation and turn herself in."

"How did she react?"

"She laughed at me. Said I had no proof that would stand up in court, that even if I did, the penalties were minimal compared to her profits."

Dr. Whitman's voice hardened. "She was proud of the destruction. She called it 'efficient resource utilization.' She said the original paintings were 'worthless damaged goods' that she'd transformed into 'valuable investment oppor-tunities.'"

"So you killed her?" Corbin said. "How did you do it?"

"I shot her with her own gun, of course. The same weapon she'd used to murder Sophia. Poetic justice, don't you think? I was amazed at how stupid the woman was. I went to the window behind her desk and stared out for a moment, then turned, pulled open the drawer, took out the gun, stepped up close and shot her in the head. Then I arranged the scene to look like suicide. It took no more than a few minutes." She smiled. "I thought I'd gotten away with it. If only I hadn't made that stupid remark."

"Tell me about Jake Williams," I said.

"I needed to know what they'd done with Sophia's body, so I went to confront him. He denied everything, of course, even when I told him he could either tell me everything or I'd go to the police and tell them I saw Lisa murder Sophia. He just laughed at me and told me I couldn't prove he was even there. He was right, of course. So I looked around, and I picked up one of his tools."

"And you killed him," Corbin stated.

She shrugged. "He deserved it for what he'd done to those paintings. So yes, I took him by surprise. I stabbed him in the chest. I don't think he even felt the first blow. He grabbed the tool, but it was covered in blood, and his hands slipped off it. I was panicking by then. He wasn't a small man, you know. But I managed to stab him two more times before he went down. I was surprised at how quickly he died. I wiped the tool with a dirty rag—which I took with me—then dropped it and left."

The matter-of-fact way she described committing murder was more than a little disturbing.

"Don't you feel remorse for killing Lisa Reynolds and Jake Williams?" Corbin asked.

"I feel remorse that it was necessary. But they were committing crimes against our cultural heritage. Someone had to stop them."

"That wasn't your decision to make," he said.

"Wasn't it?" she said as she stood and walked to a window overlooking her garden. "Captain Gazzara, I want you to understand something. I've spent my entire career preserving cultural heritage. I've restored paintings that were damaged by wars, accidents, and the simple passage of time. I've saved artwork that might otherwise have been lost forever."

She turned back to face us. "But Lisa Reynolds and Jake Williams weren't preserving anything. They were systematically destroying irreplaceable pieces of human cultural memory for criminal profit. There are no photographs of the period. All we have are the paintings. They had to be stopped."

I heaved a sigh. I'd heard enough. I stood up and said. "I understand what you're saying, Dr. Whitman, but you can't go around murdering people. Do you have anything else to say before we take you in?"

"May I pack a few things?"

"I'm afraid not," I said. "We need to go now."

As we led Dr. Whitman to our cars, I couldn't help but note the irony of it. Here was someone who'd dedicated her life to preserving cultural treasures, who'd committed murder to protect art from destruction. Her methods were criminal, but her motives touched on the fundamental question about society's obligation to preserve our irreplaceable heritage.

The Painted Lady was gone forever, but we finally had the answers we needed. Dr. Patricia Whitman had appointed herself judge, jury, and executioner in the service of cultural preservation.

Whether that made her a criminal or a crusader would be for the courts to decide.

10

JUSTICE AND MEMORY

AFTER SEVERAL DAYS OF SEARCHING, THEY FOUND SOPHIA Blake's body in a shallow grave at the edge of the landfill. The person who buried her there was never found, though we all knew it had been someone Jake Williams had hired following Lisa's orders. The recovery gave her family closure, but it also served as a grim reminder of how far Lisa Reynolds had been willing to go to protect her profits.

Sophia's memorial service took place on a frosty January morning at Riverside Cemetery six months after the conclusion of the case. Dr. Patricia Whitman wasn't there. She was serving a life sentence at the Debra K. Johnson Rehabilitation Center in Nashville.

I stood with Samson at the edge of the gathering, watching as Dr. Patterson delivered a eulogy that emphasized Sophia's dedication to cultural preservation and historical truth. The crowd included faculty from the university, members of the art community, law enforcement colleagues, and even some of Father Blake's students. It was a good turnout for a young woman whose only crime had been pursuing the truth.

"Sophia Blake died defending our cultural heritage," Patterson said. "Her research exposed the systematic vandalism of irreplaceable artwork, and her courage in pursuing the truth cost her her life. But Sophia's sacrifice wasn't in vain. Her work has resulted in lasting changes: new laws, better training, increased awareness of art fraud..." And on he droned.

Michelle Parry did attend the service, escorted by her court-appointed supervisor. She stood apart from the main group, and she didn't look well. After the ceremony, she hesitantly approached me.

"Captain Gazzara, I think about Sophia every day when I'm at work. I want you to know how sorry I am for what I did, and that I'm working hard, trying to honor her memory by protecting the kind of artwork I helped destroy."

Michelle's rehabilitation had been genuine. She'd received thirty-six months in the county jail with the opportunity for outwork and, over the past eight months, she'd worked on legitimate restoration projects at several museums, always under supervision, always wearing an electronic ankle bracelet that reminded everyone—including herself—of her past crimes.

"I'll never forgive myself for my role in destroying those paintings," she said. "But I'm grateful for the opportunity to redirect my skills."

"The past is the past, Michelle," I replied. "The paintings are gone, and beating yourself up won't bring them back. What matters now is what you do going forward." It was a trite response, I know. But no matter what she said, she knew what she was doing when she created those forgeries. Still, people deserved second chances when they were willing to earn them.

There was no trial for Dr. Whitman. Her attorney had managed to talk the prosecution down from first-degree in return for a guilty plea, arguing that the murders hadn't been premeditated but rather crimes of passion triggered by witnessing horrifying cultural destruction. She pleaded guilty to two counts of second-degree murder.

The plea deal had been controversial. District Attorney Morrison had initially pushed for first-degree charges, but Dr. Whitman's clean record, her cooperation with the investigation, and the unusual circumstances had ultimately swayed the prosecution toward accepting the lesser charges. The defense had argued successfully that witnessing Sophia's murder had triggered something in Dr. Whitman that transformed her from preservationist to vigilante.

During sentencing, Dr. Whitman had shown little remorse. She stood before Judge Harrison with the same composed demeanor she'd maintained throughout the investigation, as if she were delivering a lecture rather than facing judgment.

"I would make the same choices again," she'd told the judge. "Lisa Reynolds and Jake Williams destroyed irreplaceable cultural treasures. I didn't set out to kill either of them. I'm not a violent person. It just happened. But for what they did to those paintings, for the centuries of history they scraped away for profit..."

She'd trailed off, but her meaning was clear. In her mind, their deaths were justified by their crimes.

Judge Harrison had been visibly frustrated by her lack of remorse. "Dr. Whitman, regardless of your motives or the provocation you felt, two people are dead by your hand. The court cannot overlook that fact."

He'd paused, reviewing his notes before continuing. "I've struggled with this case more than any other in my twenty-three years on the bench. Your dedication to preserving history and culture is admirable. Your professional reputation is exemplary. Everyone who knows you speaks of your integrity and your devotion to your work. But you took two lives, Dr. Whitman. Two human lives. You appointed yourself judge, jury, and executioner. No cause, however righteous, justifies taking the law into your own hands."

The judge had looked directly at her. "Our legal system exists precisely to prevent individuals like you from doing that, no matter how noble they believe their cause to be. If we allow passion to override law, we have chaos, not civilization."

He'd sentenced her to twenty years to life on each count, to be served concurrently, with eligibility for parole after twenty years. "Dr. Whitman," he'd said, "you will have considerable time to think about your actions and their consequences. I hope you use that time to reflect upon the difference between justice and revenge, and perhaps find some genuine remorse for the lives you took."

Her sentence had been controversial in some circles, but law enforcement emphasized the importance of maintaining the legal process even when dealing with sympathetic motives. Dr. Whitman had become a cautionary tale about what happened when good intentions collided with an obsessive personality and a willingness to take extreme action.

The case had prompted significant changes beyond just the sentences handed down. The systematic destruction of artwork had indeed led to new legislation, which increased penalties for art fraud and provided funding for authentication research. Museums and galleries nationwide had implemented new protocols for verifying artwork provenance and detecting sophisticated forgeries.

Vincent Harper was never found. Despite extensive searches and federal involvement, the freelance authenticator who'd helped certify the forgeries simply vanished. Some believed he'd used his $20,000 cash withdrawal to disappear into a new identity somewhere far from Chattanooga. Others suspected he'd met the same fate as Lisa and Jake, his body hidden where it would never be discovered. The truth died with Dr. Whitman's silence. She refused to discuss Harper during any of her interviews, leaving his disappearance as one of the case's enduring mysteries.

Marcus Webb had emerged from the scandal with his reputation intact, but with his collection reduced significantly. Of the twelve pieces he'd purchased from Lisa's gallery, seven were worthless forgeries. Despite losing over two million dollars, Webb remained philosophical about his losses.

"I wanted to preserve Southern art history but unknowingly funded its destruction," he told me during our final interview. "Maybe some good can come from this tragedy. At least I hope it will, but you know people better than I do, Captain. Maybe I'm naïve. Maybe it's a forlorn hope."

I smiled at him—it was all I could think of—put my hand on his arm, showed him out of the building, and thanked him, though I wondered after exactly what I'd thanked him for.

Webb donated his remaining authentic pieces to the Hunter Museum and established the Marcus Webb Foundation for Cultural Preservation, funding authentication research and graduate student projects. His foundation had already begun working with law enforcement agencies to develop better training programs for recognizing art fraud.

Carmen Rodriguez's insurance investigation had led to federal involvement across eight states, with total damages estimated at over thirty million dollars. The FBI's Art Crime Team took over the broader investigation, and law enforcement agencies nationwide received training in recognizing art fraud.

Grace Parker's blog gained national attention, establishing her as a respected voice in the art world. Despite job offers from major publications, she remained in Chattanooga to continue investigating art crimes in the Southeast. Her persistence had been instrumental in tracking down leads that helped federal investigators prosecute other members of the forgery network.

"Sophia Blake started this investigation," Grace said during one of our last conversations. "The least I can do is continue her work." It was a nice sentiment, but I couldn't help but wonder if continuing Sophia's work might lead Grace down the same dangerous path. So, I made sure she understood the risks and had my contact information.

A year after Dr. Whitman's sentencing, I received my first letter from her. Even from her cell, she continued to provide information about potential art fraud cases, as if prison were just another workplace where she could pursue her mission of cultural preservation. And there was more of the same in subsequent letters. Her obsession hadn't dimmed one iota despite her circumstances. If anything, having unlimited time to think had intensified her focus on what she saw as crimes against humanity.

I had little sympathy for her, so I'd responded briefly, acknowledging her cooperation while maintaining that what she'd done was inexcusable, no matter her motives. Murder was murder, regardless of how noble the killer believed their cause to be.

During a law enforcement conference the following year, when asked whether I thought Dr. Whitman's sentence was proportionate given her motives, I replied: "She committed murder twice. Her motives, pure though they may have been, don't change the fundamental nature of her crimes. If we make exceptions for people who think their causes justify murder, we undermine the entire legal framework that protects all of us."

The questions the case raised remained as relevant as ever, and they cut to the heart of how our system of justice should work. How do we protect irreplaceable cultural treasures—or people for that matter—when the penalties seem so laughably small? How do we balance individual action with institutional responsibility when bureaucracy moves too slowly? How do we ensure that passion for legitimate causes doesn't transform good people into vigilantes?

These questions didn't have simple answers, but they were worth asking, I suppose. The Painted Lady represented more than an expensive painting. It represented one man's impulse to create, remember, and preserve the things that define our civilization. In destroying it for profit, Lisa and Jake had committed a crime that went beyond fraud— they'd erased a piece of history that could never be recovered.

Me? I had no answers. I'm just a simple cop who tries to catch the bad guys and hopes the system will sort out the rest.

THANK you for reading this short story. I hope you enjoyed this novella, The Painted lady with Kate Gazzara.

IF YOU WOULD LIKE to read more books with Kate check out my Kate Gazzara Murder Files. You can jump in anywhere or start at the beginning. Keep reading for a full list of my books!

WAYS TO GET NOTIFIED FOR NEW RELEASES:

FOLLOW ON AMAZON, BOOKBUB, AND JOIN THE AUTHORS EMAIL LIST.

SIGN UP For Announcements & great deals from the author on his website!
Visit www.BlairHowardBooks.com

Don't forget to confirm your email and whitelist (save as contact)BlairHoward@blairhowardbooks.com to your email system.

Short Stories and Novellas

Buried Secrets(Harry Starke)

The Painted Lady(Kate Gazzara)

Stand Alone

Hunter's Moon(Kate & Harry)

Series

The Harry Starke Genesis Series

9 Books in Series as of 2025

The Harry Starke Series

25 Books in Series as of 2025

The Lt. Kate Gazzara Murder Files

22 Books in Series as of 2025

Randall And Carver Mysteries

4 Books in Series as of 2025

The Peacemaker Series

3 Books in Series as of 2025

The O'Sullivan Chronicles: Civil War Series

5 Books in Series as of 2025

Science Fiction From Blair C. Howard

The Sovereign Star Series

7 Books in Series as of 2025

also available in German

The Predecessors Series

The Last Station-Book One

The Infinity War-Book Two